DESTINY'S
CHILD

DESTINY'S CHILD

Iris Gower

G.K. Hall & Co. • Chivers Press
Thorndike, Maine USA   Bath, England

This Large Print edition is published by G.K. Hall, USA,
and by Chivers Press, England.

Published in 1999 by arrangement with Severn House Publishers Ltd.

U.S. Hardcover   0-7838-8768-X (Romance Series Edition)
U.K. Hardcover   0-7540-3965-X (Chivers Large Print)
U.K. Softcover   0-7540-3966-8 (Camden Large Print)

Originally published 1975 under the title *Bride of the Thirteenth Summer*
and pseudonym *Iris Davies*.

The text of this Large Print edition is unabridged.
Other aspects of the book may vary from the original edition.
Set in 16 pt. Plantin by Al Chase.

Printed in the United States on permanent paper.

Library of Congress Cataloging-in-Publication Data
Gower, Iris.
    Destiny's child / Iris Gower.
       p.   cm.
    ISBN 0-7838-8768-X (lg. print : hc : alk. paper)
    1. Beaufort, Margaret, Countess of Richmond and Derby,
1443–1509 — Fiction.   2. Great Britain — History — War of the
Roses, 1455–1485 — Fiction.   3. Henry VII, King of England,
1457–1509 — Family — Fiction.   4. Large type books.   I. Title.
PR6057.O845D47   1999
    823'.91421—dc21   99-041963

DESTINY'S CHILD

CHAPTER ONE

The warm sunshine spread tantalising fingers of light into the bedchamber, illuminating the brilliant silk of the tapestries and carrying the scent of early flowers to where Margaret stood obediently still.

"The gown suits you tolerably well, my child." Her mother, the Duchess of Somerset, stood, head on one side, considering her daughter with careful eyes. "Now let us place the collar of rubies to see the full effect."

Margaret hated rubies. She disliked the colour red in any shape or form, but her opinion was not sought in the matter. The gold was heavy around her throat and the gleaming stones dazzled her eyes as the sun struck fire from their redness.

She wondered impatiently how much longer it would be before she was free to run outside on to the soft grass and breathe the sweet air.

"Try not to look so discontent, Margaret." Her mother's voice held a touch of humour as she leaned forward to adjust the fur that edged the heavy gown.

Margaret felt the colour rise to her face and she moved restlessly under her mother's hands, longing to throw off the rich, heavy clothes and the choking gold collar and return to the freedom of her simple linen gown.

The Duchess returned to her chair and smiled her approval.

"Yes, I think you will do very well. But do try to smile! You are going to the Court of King Henry the Sixth, not to a burial!"

Margaret looked down at her shoes encrusted with gems and resisted the temptation to kick them across the room. Her mother must not be angered, especially not now when she was great with child.

The Duchess leaned back and smiled. "You will be the finest lady there, Margaret, a credit to the House of Somerset and a joy to your dear guardian." She pressed the tips of her white fingers together. "I will expect William de la Pole to make a great marriage for you, even though he has not taken his wardship very seriously until now."

Margaret shuddered delicately at the thought of her guardian and touched the cold gems in the collar which had been his present to her. William, Duke of Suffolk, was a man to fear. He had tight, mean lips and familiar hands.

"Do I really have to leave Bletsoe, mother?" she asked, and in spite of herself, her voice trembled.

"Come now, Margaret," her mother spoke kindly, "you are almost nine years of age. Time you learned a little of what womanhood is all about. You cannot forever shelter behind your mother's skirts." She lifted her hand and beckoned to one of her ladies. "Elizabeth, help my daughter to disrobe. I think she has put up with enough for one day."

She rose and went to the door of the chamber, smiling graciously at her daughter.

"Be sure to present yourself early in the great hall. We must not keep William waiting. He will be eager to see how you have grown." She paused for a moment and regarded Margaret with steady eyes. "It would be well to remember that my lord of Suffolk is perhaps the most powerful minister in the realm. You must do your best to please him so that he will take good care of you at court."

Margaret nodded her assent and, satisfied of her daughter's sense of duty, the Duchess left the room.

"Help me out of these things quickly, Elizabeth!" Margaret plucked at the hated collar and threw it on to the bed where it lay among the covers like a pool of rich blood.

Elizabeth removed the garments with deft fingers, smiling her affection.

"Don't take on so, Margaret. You will make yourself overheated if you carry on like that." She brought a bowl of rosewater and placed it on the table. "Let me bathe your head. You will soon feel better."

Margaret sat quietly enjoying the scented coolness and relaxing under Elizabeth's ministrations.

"Have you always known me, Elizabeth?" she asked after a time, and Elizabeth laughed out loud.

"Good gracious, yes. I was present at your birth! I heard your first cry and saw you placed among the rich tapestries of your crib. A tiny delicate girl you were."

Margaret wriggled her toes a little and attempted to pluck up courage to ask Elizabeth the one question she dare not ask her mother.

"Is it true my father died by his own hand?" The words came out suddenly.

Elizabeth did not conceal her surprise. "My dear girl, where have you heard such a thing?" She busied herself at the table and Margaret noticed that her hands were trembling.

"It is true, isn't it?" Margaret persisted. "Please tell me. I can't bear *not* to know."

Elizabeth sighed. "Very well. It seems as though the Duke of Somerset killed himself because he fell into ill favour with the King; but no one is sure. It could easily have been an accident."

Margaret brushed back a stray curl impatiently and pushed Elizabeth away when she attempted to place the cool cloth on her brow once more.

"My mother couldn't have loved him very well," she said quietly. "She didn't mourn for long before she married Leo."

Elizabeth looked scandalized. "My dear Margaret, that is really not the way to talk about your mother and Lord Wells. Did you expect her to remain alone without a husband to take care of her?"

Margaret bowed her head and considered the question very carefully.

"I wish to marry someone whom I can love with all my heart, and I shall make sure he is too happy to ever take his own life."

She chewed her thumbnail, her wide eyes so innocent and trusting, that Elizabeth felt tears come to her own eyes. Quickly she made the sign of the cross.

"I pray that life may treat you with kindness, Margaret. But none can say what lies before us."

She tidied away the bowl and pulled the covers of Margaret's bed neatly into place.

"Try to rest now," she said gently. "Your mother expects you to be at your brightest this evening. And don't forget, once you are at Court many people will flatter you and wish to introduce you to their eligible sons. You must keep your head set on the right way, and don't become too proud."

Margaret's eyes brightened with interest. "Why should they do that? Surely everyone at the King's Court must be wealthy already?"

Elizabeth nodded knowingly. "That may be so, but no one is so rich that they don't try to accumulate more riches; and you are a great heiress. A catch for anyone."

Margaret sighed suddenly. "It is a great pity that my father did not live, then I would not have to go with my Lord of Suffolk."

Elizabeth moved to the door. "You haven't much to complain of. Your mother has more than done her duty. Why, see how well you can read. Even those funny French writings are intelligible to you."

Margaret sat on her bed and wound thin arms around her knees.

"Yes, I have a lot to be grateful for, and I will do my best to be good," she said humbly.

Elizabeth choked back her tears. How young and vulnerable Margaret was. A small, unformed girl, who would soon be thrust into the decadent life at Court. Suddenly a thought sprang into her mind. What if she should seek permission to go with Margaret? Surely the Duchess would be pleased with such an idea.

Silently she left the room. It would do no good to mention her plan yet as it might well come to nothing, and then Margaret would be disappointed.

The great hall rang with the sound of many voices and wine flowed like a river of blood, filling cups almost before they were empty.

Margaret shook her head as a servant offered her more meat. Her stomach knotted so that she could not even eat the light almond sweets that she loved so much.

At her side, towering over the proceedings like a bearded giant, sat William, Duke of Suffolk, his small eyes constantly lit with some inner amusement, resting on her now and again as if he saw not the Lady Margaret Beaufort but a shining pile of gold pieces.

On his other side was his son John, a thin boy who blushed every time anyone looked his way.

Margaret felt even more sorry for him than she did for herself. After all, he had spent his life with the Duke and from his pale appearance, it had not so far been a happy one.

She leaned over and offered him a rosy apple. He glanced at her nervously, and shook his head. She persisted, and at last he held out a tentative hand and took it.

The Duchess of Somerset intercepted the little pantomime and leaned forward, smiling indulgently.

"Your son seems to like Margaret very well, William," she said. "And I'm sure you are bound to agree that Margaret has become quite a little beauty, has she not?"

William laughed out loud and Margaret flinched, her colour rising.

"It will be a long time before she will be as lovely as you, Duchess," he said loudly.

Margaret glanced at Leo to see how he would take the Duke's familiarity, but there was nothing but pride on Lord Wells' face as if he heartily agreed that his wife was the most lovely woman in all the kingdom.

Suddenly Margaret jumped as the Duke of Suffolk rested his hot hand on her shoulder.

"Nevertheless, I think little Margaret will be a fine woman in a few years time. Maybe even make a bride for my son John. It is a possibility to keep in mind."

Margaret looked quickly away from John's face, but not before he'd winked secretly at her.

She stared down at her hands as they rested in her lap. Perhaps marriage with John would be quite pleasant so long as his father did not live close to them.

She glanced at him again from beneath her lashes, relieved that at least he did not repel her as did his father. He seemed kindly disposed to her and she was sure that he would not subject her to the fumbling intimacies that the Duke of Suffolk imposed upon her.

At that moment the Duke turned to face her, almost as if he could read her mind.

"I see you like the small trinket I brought you." His hand caressed her throat in a pretence of looking at the rubies, and Margaret sat perfectly still, feeling like a bird of prey with a hawk about to swoop on it.

Somehow she managed to make a polite reply, but when she would have looked away, the Duke forced her chin up so that her eyes met his.

"You are a tender little bud, Margaret, but you will be well nurtured in the House of Suffolk. Remember always that I am a man of substance. Why, the King dare not make a single move without my approval."

Margaret wondered what she was supposed to say, and at last she simply attempted a nod, hoping to dislodge the Duke's fingers from their hold.

"My dear William, the child is but nine years

of age. Don't expect to put too wise a head on young shoulders. It would not be right."

The Duchess of Somerset leaned forward and gently tapped his hand so the Duke withdrew his hold. Margaret turned a grateful glance towards her mother, but it seemed she was already engrossed in something her husband was saying.

John de la Pole bit into his apple and his eyes twinkled at Margaret. She smiled, warming to him, thinking it a great pity that he was not tall and handsome as she had always imagined her husband would be. Still, he had a kind face, and seemed to be as bored with the proceedings as she was.

He offered her an almond sweetmeat and she took it merely to please him, smiling in delight as he made a disrespectful grimace behind his father's broad back. Life at Court might not be so bad after all, she decided, as the soft comfit melted deliciously against her teeth.

Margaret sat stiffly in her chair watching Elizabeth pack away the last of her clothes into a chest. Now that the moment of departure had really come, she could only think of how she would miss her mother and the kindly Leo and how she would never again run barefoot across the sweet grass of Bletsoe.

"Cheer up," Elizabeth said briskly, noticing her long face. "I'll be with you, so there's no need to be frightened." She smiled warmly and patted Margaret's cheek. "I think it was exceedingly kind of your mother to allow me to go to Court with you. See how she cares about your well-being."

Margaret tried to smile in return, but the foolish tears brimmed into her eyes and it seemed there was nothing to do to stop them flooding down her cheeks.

Quickly she left her seat and crossed to the window, looking longingly out at the rolling Bedfordshire fields.

"What if I never come home again?" she said brokenly. "What if I never see my mother and Leo, Lord Wells, and have to spend the rest of my life among strangers?"

She leaned her chin against the cool window ledge and bit her lips to stop them from trembling. If her mother should see her in such a state of distress, she would be very displeased at her loss of dignity.

Elizabeth watched her for a moment in silence, tears very near her own eyes. Margaret was a child of nine years of age, dressed in woman's clothing and trying to think like a woman. It was a great pity that she could not remain sheltered here at Bletsoe for another few years at least. As it was, she would enter the court life still with the roundness of childhood in her face.

Margaret straightened and moved purposefully into the room, the tears drying on her cheeks.

"Mother has taught me to speak and act like a lady," she said firmly. "I must not let her down after all. Am I not highly educated so as to be a fitting wife for any man?" She squared her slender shoulders and, unable to say any more, turned her face away.

Elizabeth took her warmly in her arms, disregarding for once the strict code of behaviour that was usually observed at Bletsoe.

"There, there, don't fret; everything will be new and exciting at Court. You will meet King Henry, an honour which is not given to many young ladies."

Margaret clung for a moment and then drew herself away, nodding her head seriously.

"I am fully aware of the honour, believe me, Elizabeth. I am sure the King is as saintly as everyone says he is. It's just sad to leave my home, that's all."

"That is a perfectly natural feeling," Elizabeth said brightly, returning to her packing. "I even feel pangs of regret myself. Bletsoe is such a beautiful place. But each of us must move on to new experiences. Time will not stand still for anyone."

She searched her mind for something that would distract Margaret from her tears.

"At least there will be new books for you to read at Court. And wonderful musicians to listen to."

Margaret's face brightened. "Yes, I will enjoy reading the King's books." She smiled a little through her tears. "You always think of something pleasant, Elizabeth. I am grateful to you."

She put her arm for a moment around Elizabeth's ample waist.

"And if I am lonely in the night, I can call on you to keep me company, can I not?"

Elizabeth nodded, her throat constricted with unshed tears.

"I will always be at hand if you should need me," she said at last. "Even when you become a married lady, I will stay with you. I love you as if you were my own child."

They stood in silence for a moment and then Margaret gently disengaged herself.

"I had better go and make my farewells."

She took a deep breath and walked out into the long corridor trying to think of the excitement her new life would bring and not of the deep feeling of loss that was growing within her. As her mother so frequently told her, it did not become the daughter of the Duke of Somerset to behave with anything less than perfect control.

Her mother was sitting in the great hall with Leo attentive as always at her side. She did not rise when Margaret stood before her. She could not; she was cumbersome now with child. Instead, she crooked her bejewelled finger indicating that Margaret stand beside her and receive her brief kiss.

"I will miss you, Margaret," she said softly, and indeed she would. She had spent nine years in grooming her daughter so that she could take her rightful place among the great and wealthy of the land. After all, the Somersets were of royal blood. She took Margaret's hands, still small and plump like a baby's, into her own white elegant fingers.

"Partings are always sad," she said gently, "but the Duke of Suffolk is your rightful guardian appointed by the King to look after you and guide you always. You must obey the Duke in everything, and he will see that you have such wonderful opportunities at Court that will dazzle even your sensible mind."

She paused for a moment, regarding her daughter with something like anxiety in her eyes.

"When you are older, Margaret, you will see that sending you away to court is the best thing a mother could do for a beloved daughter, though it may seem cruel to you now. It would be selfish of me to keep you here, though that is my instinct and my wish. I must sacrifice personal feelings for your own interests, try to remember that, Margaret."

Leo stepped forward and smiled down at Margaret, his pleasant face full of affection for his tiny step-daughter.

"I am coming with you, to see you safely at Court," he said, and Margaret felt a deep gratitude to the only father she had ever known.

"Thank you, it is a great kindness," she said graciously and had the pleasure of seeing her mother smile with approval.

"Goodbye, mother. I will try to remember all you have told me."

The Duchess held her daughter for a moment

in an uncharacteristic rush of affection, and then waved her away.

"Go, child, before we all set to weeping and disgrace ourselves."

Margaret never knew how she made her way down the steps and on to the soft green grass of Bletsoe where her retinue waited ready for the journey. Her eyes were misted and her throat ached with tears she would not shed.

She looked back for a moment at the rugged walls of her home and thought she saw the bright jewel colour of her mother's dress against a window, but she could not be sure.

She turned her face away then from all that she loved, and it suddenly seemed as if her childhood had come to an abrupt end before she was fully nine years of age.

CHAPTER TWO

The heat was almost unbearable and the noise of hundreds of voices seemed to beat around Margaret with an almost physical force so that she longed to turn and run from the great hall.

The Duke of Suffolk, however, had no such thoughts, and he made a pathway with ease through the press of ladies in jewel-encrusted dresses and men who all seemed to be wearing a belt of tiny bells that jangled with complete lack of harmony whenever any of them moved.

Then they were before the throne of King Henry the Sixth and Margaret's heart fluttered with fear. What if he shall fail to speak to her, or wave her from his presence without any interest at all? Her mother would be bitterly disappointed in her daughter and would not hesitate to show it.

But incredibly, the King in his scarlet and purple robes, was smiling down at her with kindness in his pale watery eyes.

"You are welcome to our court, Lady Margaret," he said gently. "Your father, the Duke of Somerset, was our good cousin, and for his sake we will care for and protect you."

She looked up at him with awe, aware of his goodness as if he wore it like a mantle of gold around him. Many whispered that he was weak, some even hinted at a taint of madness, but at this, her first encounter with the King of England, Margaret knew only that she trusted him.

She was drawn aside then by the firm hand of her guardian and as he stepped up to the throne and leaned forward to consult with the King, she found herself almost hidden by the rich velvet skirts of the court ladies.

It was almost too much for her senses to absorb at once and she wondered if she would ever become used to the smell of heavily spiced foods mingled with the strange perfumes that emanated from the ladies surrounding her.

At home, her mother only brought out the exquisite family jewels on special occasions, but here it was commonplace to see girdles and collars of the most enormous magnificence flash and sparkle, making the most modestly dressed look like some gorgeous peacock.

The throng of ladies around Margaret suddenly parted and with a dart of fear she saw the heavy bearded face of the Duke of Suffolk bending over her.

"There you are, my lady," he said with unusual joviality. "Isn't she a little beauty? Come, tell me what you all think of my ward."

Margaret felt her colour rise as those nearest turned and regarded her with curious prying eyes. She managed to stand still and return the looks with dignity.

"A typical arrogant Somerset," someone whispered, and Margaret turned to look with cool dislike at the lady who immediately turned away.

The Duke laughed loud and drew Margaret away from the crowded chamber and out into the comparative seclusion of the long corridor.

"What is it you wish to see me about, my lord?" She pressed her hands together in an effort to stop them trembling.

The Duke moved closer to her. "You seem a little pale, my child. You are not ill, I trust?"

His tone held a note of censure, and Margaret was quick to reassure him.

"I am not ill, my Lord Suffolk, just a little tired from the long journey," she said with dignity. A smile broke through the anger on the Duke's face.

"That's the spirit! You have to be strong to bear many fine sons if you are to marry into the de la Pole family."

He leaned back against the wall, his hand still gripping her arm.

"If only your father had lived to retain the title, how much more suitable it would have been; but no matter, you have inherited the noble blood and perhaps more important, much of the lands and monies of the Somerset family — enough for me to be content."

Margaret tried to draw away, wishing fervently that some other family had aroused the Duke's interest.

"May I have your permission to retire to my chamber, my Lord Suffolk?" she said quietly. "I am very tired."

He looked down at her and smiled, though

there was no warmth in his expression.

"Yes, you may leave me in just a moment. But first, tell me what you think of court life. Does it please you?"

He leaned towards her and she could smell a mingling of wine and spice on his breath. He placed his arm against the wall behind her, effectively imprisoning her, and she stood still, a feeling of dread rising within her.

"You had better grow up a little and become more warm-blooded, my lady, otherwise you will get no de la Pole heirs." The Duke threw back his great head and laughed loudly.

Margaret searched for something to say so that the Duke would let her go on her way, but her mind was a blank of fear.

Just at that moment, Elizabeth came along the corridor, her shrewd eyes taking in the situation.

"My lord," she said, sweeping into a curtsey. "I beg your pardon, but I promised the Duchess of Somerset that I would care for her daughter and ensure she retires to her bed at a reasonable hour. Shall she come along with me now?"

With a look of displeasure, the Duke straightened, leaving Margaret free to breathe in the heady sense of relief.

He ignored Elizabeth, turning his back towards her; then the Duke spoke angrily to Margaret.

"I will expect you at my chambers in the morning." He turned away, and brushed past both of them without a backward glance.

"I wish to go to bed," Margaret said wearily. "This day has seemed such a long and eventful one, I can hardly take in any more sensations. My head swims with them as it is."

"There, my sweet pea," Elizabeth took her arm consolingly, "the Duke has frightened you. But I'm sure he means no harm. He just doesn't realise what a child you are."

Margaret glanced up at her and her eyes held such a sombre look that Elizabeth felt her heart beat fast with pity.

"Do not concern yourself. I know that I am a woman now and must learn to take care of myself." She patted Elizabeth's hand. "You may not always be near to guard me against the Duke."

Elizabeth looked away. It was a sad world when a child must learn such things at so tender an age, but there was a great deal of wisdom in what Margaret said.

"May the good Lord and all the saints protect you," she said quietly, and made the sign of the cross above Margaret's bowed head.

John de la Pole was pleasant company. Margaret liked his quick laugh and the sensitivity in his face. She guessed him to be about the same age as herself, though she felt infinitely older and wiser than him.

He too seemed to be a little frightened of his father. She could tell by the way his eyes narrowed whenever Suffolk was near. She wondered if perhaps a little of her own fear had communicated itself to him.

"Would you like to come riding with me this morning?" he asked warmly. "Father promised to take us if the weather was fine."

Margaret was at a loss. Riding with John through the crisp sunshine was a tempting prospect, but it was clouded by the thought of the Duke of Suffolk's presence.

He caught her hand. "Please say you'll come, Margaret, otherwise my father will be angry." He smiled at her disarmingly and she weakened.

"All right, John, I will come. But promise you'll stay near me."

"That is an easy promise to keep." John's boyish innocence touched Margaret and she smiled at him, brushing a speck of dust from his velvet coat.

"What a pretty scene!" The Duke of Suffolk stood in the doorway of the large chamber watching them, a strange smile on his face. "Oh, please do not allow my presence to discomfort you," he said as Margaret moved away from John. "I think you will make a handsome pair."

"Father, Margaret had consented to come riding with us," John said quickly, and she knew he was aware of her embarrassment.

"Good!" The Duke nodded in satisfaction. "The more you are seen together, the better, as far as I am concerned." He clapped his hands so suddenly that Margaret jumped. "Come then, get yourselves dressed and ready. We will ride out before the sun disappears behind the clouds."

To Margaret's relief, the Duke barely glanced at her as they rode along the quiet country tracks. He had eyes for no one but his son John, and Margaret had to admit that the boy rode well.

Once he spurred his horse forward as if he would gallop ahead, but then he returned to Margaret's side, his face rosy from the fresh breeze, his eyes sparkling.

"I almost forgot my promise to you," he said softly, "but not quite. Am I forgiven?"

Margaret laughed, enjoying the exhilaration of the ride and pleased with John because he'd returned to her side.

"Do you wish to be my wife?" John said, with a quick glance at his father's broad back. "I would take good care of you and love you always."

Margaret felt the colour rise to her cheeks. So this was why the Duke had been so eager for her to ride with them, and why he had left them both to their own devices while he rode on ahead.

"I don't know, John," she said firmly. "What would my mother think of a betrothal between us? I should have to consult with her on such an important matter."

"Of course, I understand that," John said cheerfully, "but what of your own feelings? I know you like me."

Margaret sighed, perplexed, wondering why all the joy seemed to have gone from the day.

"I will let you know my answer when I have considered well on the matter."

John teased and coaxed her, trying to make her give him at least some hint of her feelings, but Margaret remained adamant, knowing instinctively that such serious affairs were not settled as easily as John seemed to think.

At last he grew impatient. "Oh, Margaret! You are so silly and slow. Both our parents wish for us to marry, so why must you hesitate?"

She had no answer and she was relieved when the Duke swung his mount around and headed back towards home.

Margaret was sitting in the dying rays of the sun's light picking out flowers in blue silk on her tapestry work. She had not seen John for some days and wondered if he were sulking because of her refusal to answer him concerning the marriage proposal.

The door of the chamber opened suddenly, startling her out of her reverie, and Elizabeth, eyes shining with excitement, hurried into the room.

"The King spoke to me!" she said, the words tumbling over themselves with excitement. "He asked about you, Margaret. He wishes to see you at a time when it is convenient." She laughed at Margaret's startled expression. "Come along. Don't sit there as if you've lost your wits! Let me help you to put on your prettiest dress and your finest jewels."

Margaret put down her needle carefully. "You are right, Elizabeth, it would not be right to keep the King waiting."

Under the deft, quick hands of Elizabeth, Margaret was soon ready to go before the King. With a calm dignity that made her look older than her years, she walked along the corridors and into the great hall.

It seemed that most of the Court was gathered there, the ladies fanning themselves against the hot evening air and the musicians playing loudly in order to be heard above the babble of voices.

Margaret threaded her way with difficulty to the throne where the King sat, head in hands, oblivious to all around him, even his young vivacious Queen, who sat tapping her foot in time to the music.

Margaret dropped into a gracious curtsey as her mother had taught her and Queen Margaret of Anjou nodded pleasantly to her before giving her attention once more to the musicians.

Henry chanced to look up and seeing Margaret kneeling before him, rose quickly and took her by the hand.

"Come, child, away from this clamour," he said, and Margaret, her heart beating fast, followed him into his private chamber.

Margaret, though used to the grandeur of Bletsoe, had never seen such rich drapes or brilliant tapestries as those that were before her now.

"Be seated child," Henry said kindly. "I will

not keep you long."

Margaret inclined her head. "I am your honest subject, your Majesty."

She thought for a moment that a slight smile hovered around his lips, but then he was talking to her upon a serious matter.

"I understand the Duke of Suffolk would have you marry his son?" He looked at her steadily, waiting for her answer.

"That is so, your Majesty," Margaret said breathlessly. "John de la Pole asked me only the other day to be his wife."

The King appraised her with pale eyes. "And what did you reply, my Lady Margaret?"

She took a deep breath. "I told him that so serious a proposal had to be carefully thought over, your Majesty. I told him I would consult my mother."

He nodded, well pleased. "I see you are a sensible young lady, so I will tell you my own plans for the daughter of the Duke of Somerset."

The King looked away over her head, and for a moment his eyes seemed to look at distant things that others could not see. Then at last he spoke.

"I wish you to marry my uterine brother, Edmund Tudor, Earl of Richmond. He is a fine young man, perhaps more than ten years your senior, but that is all to the good."

He stopped speaking and rose to his feet, fingering the heavy cross at his waist.

"I have prayed upon the matter and truly feel that the union would be blessed by God." He spun round to face her so suddenly that she was unnerved. "What do you think of the idea, Margaret Beaufort? Would you not rather the half-brother of a King than the son of my minister, Suffolk?"

"I will do what God and my King wills, your Majesty," Margaret said, and bowed her head humbly, wondering why the King should do her such an honour. He looked at her almost as if he read her thoughts.

"You have royal blood in your veins, my dear little lady, descended, as I am, from King Edward." He paused and brushed his hand over his eyes. "Added to that, there is a goodness about you, an innocence that is not often seen at the court of King Henry the Sixth, I regret to say."

He returned to his seat and rested his head against the plump cushions as if unutterably weary. Just then, the Queen swept into the room, her dark eyes bright with curiosity.

"What is keeping you away from the festivities of the Court, your Majesty?" she said, and leaned against the King with remarkable lack of respect, touching his forehead lightly with her fingers. "Have you one of your horrid headaches again?" He voice was deep and heavily accented and she turned her eyes accusingly on Margaret.

"I would like the Lady Margaret to join in marriage with my brother the Earl of Richmond," he said gently, laying his head on his young Queen's shoulder. "Do you not think it a good match?"

The Queen's dark eyes studied Margaret for a moment. "Yes, she will do well enough."

Henry looked at his Queen with respect more than love, Margaret decided, but perhaps Margaret of Anjou would be strong enough to help the King make vital decisions, and if only she could provide him with an heir, perhaps he would lose the weary, helpless look that clung to his features.

"My brother will return to Court within the next few days." The King looked more cheerful. "I will bring the two of you together and leave it to God to do the rest."

The Queen raised her eyebrows. "The good Lord helps those who help themselves, your Majesty." And there was a note of disrespect in her voice.

Henry failed to notice, and smiled down at Margaret.

"You will meet my brother Jasper too, though I don't think I shall marry him off so easily. He is an excellent soldier, but not much good at soft compliments."

The Queen took Henry's hand in her own. "You have done everything you could do for your half-brothers," she said kindly, "and for your stepfather, Owen Tudor, too. Your mother would have been proud of you, had she lived."

Margaret moved uneasily, feeling that she was eavesdropping on the King's private conversation and wondering if he had forgotten about her.

It was as if he read her thoughts again. "I will not forget my promise," he said gently. "You may withdraw and join in the festivities if you so wish."

When Margaret returned to the great hall, she was conscious of the curious stares that came her way and many of the ladies smiled at her with more friendliness than they had previously shown.

Margaret confided in Elizabeth, who smiled in delight because the King had chosen such an honour for the young Lady Margaret.

"It is only what you deserve," she said proudly. "And some of the high and mighty ladies of the Court are beginning to realise that one day you may hold great power in those tiny hands of yours."

"What did the King talk to you about, child?" The Duke of Suffolk fingered a choice piece of peacock before transferring it lazily to his bearded mouth.

Margaret stood before him, trembling. "He told me a little about his stepfather, Owen Tudor, my lord. And about his brothers, the Earls of Pembroke and Richmond."

"Ah!"

Suffolk seized her with a greasy hand and Margaret held herself still for fear of revealing how much he repelled her.

"And was marriage not mentioned?" He looked at her intently and Margaret coloured under his gaze, afraid of him and yet unwilling to speak about a matter the King had regarded as private.

"Obstinate wench!" the Duke pushed her away from him in disgust. "Go to your room, out of my sight!"

Thankfully, Margaret left him and hurried to her chamber, hoping she would encounter none of the court ladies in her headlong flight. She was in no mood for light conversation. The only thing she wanted to do at this moment was burst into tears.

She stood at her window, forcing herself to remain calm, watching how the birds swooped down among the leafy trees. How lucky they were to be free, while she was beginning to feel more like a prisoner with every passing day.

CHAPTER THREE

The hot days of summer slipped by in a profusion of new experiences, and when autumn turned the leaves of the trees to russet, Margaret felt as though she had lived all her life at the Court of Henry the Sixth.

Sometimes when she walked through the gardens she could close her eyes and picture her home at Bletsoe; but the vision was a cloudy one and after a while she no longer felt the desire to return to her old life.

She turned now towards the river, content to idle away the unexpectedly hot afternoon, strolling aimlessly over a carpet of dry crackling leaves.

"My Lady Margaret, wait!" Elizabeth was hurrying towards her, red of face and with her skirts held high in a most unladylike way.

"What on earth is wrong?" Margaret exclaimed, half in amusement, half in annoyance, that her quiet afternoon had been spoilt.

"His Majesty wishes to see you in his chambers immediately. My Lord of Suffolk brought the message, and in a good old rage he was, too."

Margaret leaned over the water, laughing at her wavering reflection.

"I have lost my chubbiness," she said in satisfaction, pinching her small cheeks.

"Yes, Margaret, but for goodness sake hurry.

You must never keep the King waiting."

Margaret rose with a sigh. "I will go to him at once."

"You will change your gown first!" Elizabeth said in horror. "That one is so plain, though I do admit the blue is very becoming to you. But you have no collar or girdle to adorn it — you could be a kitchen maid!"

"The King is not interested in my clothes," Margaret laughed wickedly. "His Queen makes certain that all his attention is focused upon her, so I hardly think he would send for me in order to admire my dress."

Margaret swept up the stairs and into the long corridor, and in a flurry of anxiety Elizabeth followed her.

The King's chamber was unusually empty so that Margaret's eyes went immediately to the tall young man with the bright, red-gold hair standing near the open window.

She dropped a deep curtsey to the King, wishing that she had listened to Elizabeth and changed into a gown more dignified and grand.

"Lady Margaret, come and meet my beloved brother, Edmund."

Margaret felt her breath leave her as she went obediently to greet the King's brother. He was a handsome man, with fire in his countenance as well as in his hair. There was a nobility of character about him that drew Margaret's senses in a way she could hardly understand.

"There, Edmund," the King said fondly,

"isn't the lady as beautiful and charming as I described her?"

As Edmund bent over to kiss Margaret's small hand, the King sat back in his chair, smiling with satisfaction. Perhaps in some way this marriage would atone to the Lady Margaret for the untimely death of her father. Henry stifled the pangs of guilt that always assailed him when he thought of the deceased Duke of Somerset. Many said he took his own life because of the way he'd bungled foreign affairs and because of his fear that he, Henry the King, might be displeased with him.

Suddenly Henry felt a mood of gloom settle upon him. "Go on out with you," he said, waving his hands towards Edmund and Margaret. "Leave me in peace."

But even when he was alone, the King could find no rest from his thoughts.

Edmund Tudor thought he had never seen anyone so lovely in the whole of his life as the young Margaret Beaufort, who now walked so demurely by his side. Her blue dress hung in simple folds around her barely ripened breasts so that she looked like a cool serene madonna.

He thought of the pleasure such a match would bring both to him and to his father, Owen Tudor, who waited back home in his Welsh castle. The Beauforts were a noble line and would mingle well with the good princely blood of the Tudors.

He felt Margaret turn and study him with large dark eyes, and it was almost as if she could look into his very thoughts.

"You are the son of a queen," she said softly. "Why should you wish to marry me?"

Edmund smiled and took her hand in his. "It is true that my mother was Queen Catherine of England, widow of Henry the Fifth, but she re-married, remember? And many at Court thought my father, a mere Welshman, was not good enough for her."

He felt Margaret's fingers curl within his own and felt her sympathy reach towards him. He longed to take her in his arms and kiss her with all the passion that stirred within him both from his Welsh father and his French mother. But she was young and fragile and he contented himself with holding her small hand to his lips for a moment.

"Don't feel sorry for me. The King is my half-brother and will care for the Tudors because it was our mother's last request."

She held on to his hand and he looked down at her, knowing that he would love her and protect her as long as he drew breath.

They walked back to the great hall in silence, not touching but as close as leaves from the same tree. Edmund stared across the green fields and some knowledge inside him told him to hold on to the happiness that burned steadily within him at this moment, because it would not be his to hold for very long.

Margaret was growing slowly into womanhood. She saw how her bodices needed to be let out to accommodate her ripening breasts, and how her waist dipped into a slender hollow, curving out to slender hips and long, thin legs.

Elizabeth noticed too. She brought a bowl of rose water to wash Margaret's long, silky hair and stared at her with sudden surprise.

"Why, here am I still thinking of you as a child and you have sprung up before my eyes like a young sapling. Look, you are almost as tall as I am."

Margaret sprinkled the cool water over her hair and tried to hide the swift colour that came to her cheeks.

"Oh, don't think I don't know what you are feeling," Elizabeth said teasingly. "I was young and in love once myself."

Margaret looked up from under the curtain of her hair, regarding the gentlewoman with new eyes.

"I cannot imagine you in love," she said, and Elizabeth shrugged her plump shoulders.

"I was young once, strange as it may seem, and if it comes to that I am not so very old now!" She rubbed at Margaret's hair vigorously.

Margaret tried to work out exactly what Elizabeth's age would be. Perhaps twenty-eight years or more. Not really old, it was true, but how much better to be in love when you were able to have your life before you to spend it with your loved one.

There was a disturbance in the outer chamber

that interrupted Margaret's pleasant thoughts of Edmund and to her dismay she heard the loud voice of the Duke of Suffolk demanding to see her. He did not wait to find if the time was convenient, but strode into the room and stood tapping a stick against his boot, his eyes appraising her.

Elizabeth quickly wrapped Margaret's hair up in a warm cloth and pulled a shawl around her slim shoulders so that she was hidden from the Duke's eager prying eyes.

"What is this I hear that you have been in the company of the Earl of Richmond in my absence?" he thundered. "Is it true?"

"Yes, my lord," Margaret said meekly. "But it is the King's wish, of that I assure you."

The Duke snorted. "Oh, yes, the King!"

Margaret felt a sudden fear that even now her guardian would find the power to over-rule the King on this matter of her marriage. He came nearer and Margaret looked up at him fearfully. He smiled unpleasantly.

"It is up to you to make a choice, my lady," he said softly. And there was a threat in his voice. "My son or the King's half-brother."

Margaret looked down at her hands, unable to speak because of the fear inside her.

"The King will not help you," the Duke said, "but I am an implacable man and I say your duty is to marry John."

Anger gave Margaret a sudden courage. "You seem to speak treason against the King, my Lord

Suffolk." Her eyes regarded him steadily and for a moment he seemed almost discomforted and then he smiled.

"Treason, my lady, is a foolish imagining in your mind." He paused. "Remember how you gave my son your word that you would marry him?"

"I promised John nothing!" she denied hotly, and the Duke raised his eyebrows.

"Well, he believes you did," he said slyly. "Are you going to deceive yourself and my son with your wayward thoughts?"

He left then and she sank down on to a stool clasping her shaking hands together.

"It is not true!" she said again in anguish. "It isn't really true." Yet even as she protested, she knew that she had at least allowed John to think that she would marry him one day.

"My lady, do not distress yourself. The Duke cannot force you into marriage. The King would not allow it."

Elizabeth helped her to her feet, and gently continued to dry her hair.

Margaret turned to her, tears stinging her eyes. "Am I bound by honour to marry John? Oh, Elizabeth, I don't know what to think!"

Elizabeth shook her head. "I cannot find you an easy solution, Margaret, but you could offer prayers to Saint Nicholas, the patron saint of all true maidens. Perhaps then you will find guidance and truth."

Margaret smiled a little. "Thank you for your

good council, Elizabeth. I will do as you say."

Margaret sat in uncomfortable silence staring across the chamber at John de la Pole. He stood next to his mother's chair, a sulky look making him seem younger than he was.

The Duchess of Suffolk spoke suddenly, startling Margaret so that the colour flew to her cheeks.

"Welcome to my home. I hope we will be great friends as well as kinsfolk," she said brightly. "You realise, of course, that I am blood cousin to the Beauforts?"

Margaret nodded politely, not knowing what to say, but the Duchess did not need an answer.

"This match between you and my son John would be fitting. You must surely see that for yourself, my dear. You are of a similar age and both of you have been carefully nurtured."

The Duke came into the room quite suddenly and went to his wife, kissing her dutifully on the cheek.

"Well, Alice, has the Lady Margaret seen sense yet?"

He glowered across at Margaret, a dark look of anger on his broad face.

His wife seemed a little anxious. "I am dealing with the matter with no recourse to raised voices, my lord," she said reproachfully, and a smile illumined his face as he bowed over her jewelled hands.

"I ask your pardon, Alice, my dear. I am a little

hasty, I see that now. Come, my Lady Margaret," he said more gently, "surely there is no problem here?"

She tried not to shake as she answered him. "I am praying for guidance, my Lord Suffolk, and though I don't wish to offend you, there is the matter of Edmund Tudor and the King's wish that I should take him as my husband."

"But my dear girl," the Duchess broke in, "surely you would prefer to marry John. He must be more to your liking than the Earl of Richmond."

Margaret heard the hurt in the Duchess's voice and she could understand it well. No mother would like to feel her son was rejected.

"I'm sorry," she said gently, "I like John very much, but I am duty bound to consider both offers with equal seriousness."

John spoke then for the first time. "It is no use to press the Lady Margaret," he said quietly. "She must be allowed to choose freely. I would not wish it otherwise."

He smiled at Margaret, and her eyes conveyed her gratitude.

"You do not know what you are about!" the Duchess said sharply. "And the King could well change his mind or lose it altogether!"

She closed her lips at a stern look from the Duke, her husband, knowing that she had gone too far.

"You would be safer marrying John," the Duke said firmly, "but we will discuss it no more today. John, show the Lady Margaret round our home. She has only seen this chamber so far and not much of that with all the talking we've done I dare say."

His hand rested for a moment on the shoulder of his son, and Margaret could see that whatever other faults he may have, he loved him dearly.

John led the way along the corridors which were chill now with the coming of winter and he looked so crestfallen that she took his hand and smiled warmly at him.

"John, don't worry even if you don't marry me. I'm sure you will some day make a very good match."

He smiled in return. "That may well be, Margaret, but I will never forget that you could have been my bride. I know now inside me that it is not meant to be."

Margaret looked at him steadily for a moment. "It is true that I want with all my heart to marry Edmund Tudor, but I don't know if it would be right, really I don't."

He looked at her in bewilderment. "But, I thought you had made up your mind as to what course to take."

She shook her head. "I don't want to make any mistakes, John, and it is sometimes hard to see what is the right thing to do."

He stood still, forgetting to show her the high arched roof of the great hall, and stared directly at her.

"Surely you must do what you know is in your

heart. Give your love to the Tudor, otherwise you may live to regret it all your life."

"Thank you, John, it is generous of you to say that. And you know what high regard I shall always have for you." She squeezed his hand. "Now let us look around your lovely home. Soon I will have to go back to Court."

John gave her a long look. "I wish things could have been different, but I wish you great happiness all the same."

He turned away, and in silence led her back to the great hall.

Although Margaret had only been away from the court for a short time, Elizabeth greeted her in a fever of excitement.

"Why, you are filling out, Margaret, though of course you will never be as plump as I am!"

Margaret caught her hands. "I am very glad to be back. It was something of an ordeal living in the same house as my guardian even for a few weeks!"

"Well?" Elizabeth demanded. "Was anything decided about the marriage?"

Margaret shook her head and laughed. "You are too inquisitive! I don't think I shall tell you!"

Elizabeth smiled with mock cunning. "In that case, I will not tell you what message my lord, the Earl of Richmond, left for you."

"Oh, Elizabeth! You must tell me or I'll never forgive you."

"He wishes to meet with you. He will come to your rooms as soon as you return."

As Elizabeth said the words, there was a heavy knocking on the door and Margaret clapped her hand over her mouth to stop the scream of excitement that trembled on her lips.

Then Edmund was at her side enfolding her in his arms, and she closed her eyes in ecstasy.

"It is so good to be back at Court, especially as you are here," she said softly, and Edmund smiled, kissing the flower of her mouth again and again.

"The King is coming this way!" Elizabeth said urgently, and Edmund released Margaret but still held her small hand in his.

Margaret dipped into a deep curtsey and the King smiled down at her.

"Charming. Like a spring flower," he said, raising her up. "My brother is a lucky man indeed to have you for his wife."

Margaret felt breathless and it was Edmund who spoke.

"You are generous, Henry, to allow the marriage to take place."

The King's pale eyes became misty. "Our lady mother would have wished you to be happy," he said emotionally, and for a moment Margaret found herself in the absurd position of pitying the King of England. He looked down forlornly at his shaking hands. "I sometimes wish I had been one of Owen Tudor's sons instead of falling heir to the crown of England through my father Henry the Fifth. You, Edmund, or indeed Jasper, would have made a far stronger King."

46

"Come," Edmund said gently, going to the King's side, "let me come with you back to your own chamber, you need to rest a little while."

The half-brothers stood for a moment under the slanting light from the windows, similar in some respects, but where the King's mouth was weak and indecisive, Edmund was firm of jaw and clear of eye.

He turned to Margaret and a smile lit up his face. "I will see you later, my lady," he said, and his eyes sent her messages that brought the rich colour into her cheeks.

When she returned to the room, Elizabeth was smiling knowingly. "There will be a marriage soon," she said happily. "Edmund, Earl of Richmond, is a man in love and as such, an impatient man."

Margaret said nothing, but she hoped in her heart that Elizabeth was right.

CHAPTER FOUR

Margaret rose from a kneeling position and winced at the sudden pain that licked like a fire along her ankles. Her back was sore and she realised it must have been three hours or more since she had first begun to pray.

Wearily she climbed between the covers and closed her eyes; tonight perhaps St Nicholas would see fit to answer her prayers.

She must have dozed for a while, because she awoke suddenly, feeling heavy-eyed and strangely disturbed. A dark mist seemed to cover the room, dimming the tapers, and then suddenly at the side of the bed Margaret saw a bishop, holding his hands over her in benediction.

Her breath caught in her throat and the sound of her own heart-beats seemed to echo around the walls. She moved a little to the farthest edge of the bed, but the figure remained where it was, as substantial as she herself.

"My daughter, I commend unto you Edmund to be your husband."

The voice was all around Margaret's head, it echoed against the tapestries and resounded hollowly among the drapes.

As she stared wide-eyed, the dark mists seemed to draw nearer until the figure of the bishop was wholly enveloped, and then she was alone in the room with the tapers once more burning brightly.

She rubbed her eyes, wondering if she had been dreaming; or was the bishop an answer to her prayers?

"Elizabeth!" she said urgently, and the gentle-woman came at once pulling on a robe over her night-shift.

"What is it, Margaret? You look so pale. I hope you have not caught a chill."

"I believe my prayers have been answered," she said softly.

Elizabeth listened in awe as Margaret told her what she had seen and quickly made the sign of the cross, her eyes searching the dark corners of the room.

"There is nothing to fear," Margaret said softly. "Saint Nicholas will not come again, you can be sure of that."

She lay back wearily and Elizabeth pulled the covers around her shoulders.

"Would you like me to sit with you a while?" Her voice trembled a little in spite of her brave words.

"No thank you, Elizabeth, I am all right. I will sleep well now."

Margaret turned her face against the bolster, her hair spreading in soft tendrils around her so that she seemed little more than a baby.

Elizabeth paused for a moment longer, tears caught in a tight knot inside her, then she quietly left the room.

"But my Lord Suffolk, I see no need to leave the Court at this time." Margaret spoke firmly, though her hands were clasped together to prevent them trembling. "The King has not directed me in any way."

The Duke looked down at her angrily. "May I remind you, my lady, that *I* am your guardian, not the King?" He tapped his foot impatiently, brushing an imaginary speck of dust from his fine cloak. "You will oblige me by making yourself ready as quickly as possible." His eyes were dark and challenging, and Margaret realised there was nothing to do but obey him.

"Is my Lady Elizabeth to go with us?" she asked hopefully; but the Duke shook his head.

"You will be well attended at my home." He sounded impatient and Margaret shrugged in resignation. She looked towards Elizabeth meaningfully.

"Convey my regrets to my friends that I shall not be seeing them this afternoon, but as soon as I return I will make up for it."

Elizabeth nodded understandingly and Margaret knew that Edmund, Earl of Richmond, would be informed of the day's events.

It was a strange, heavy day, with clouds rolling ominously over tormented skies so that beads of moisture clung like raindrops to Suffolk's face.

"Our journey is a short one," he remarked, "and a good thing too; we will no doubt arrive at my estates before the storm breaks."

Margaret made no reply. She was indifferent to the moods of the weather. She closed her eyes, imagining Edmund's anger when he discovered that Suffolk had taken her away from the Court, and in spite of her gloom, her heart glowed with love and happiness.

The Lady Alice was warm in her greeting and behind her, like a thin sapling, stood John, his face drawn and troubled. Margaret thought she could see a new maturity in him that had not been there before. He caught her arm as the Duke of Suffolk preceded them into the great hall.

"You know we are to be married?" he whispered anxiously.

Margaret stared at him in horror, her heart beating painfully fast. "It cannot be true, John. Your father would not dare to marry us without the consent of the King!"

John smiled dryly. "The King grows more and more dependent upon my father. To hold the avaricious barons at bay, I believe the King would allow him to do almost anything he chose."

Margaret's mouth was dry. "I don't wish to be married to anyone yet. I am too young. Surely, John, your father could arrange a more advantageous match for you?"

He shrugged. "I know nothing of that, but I do know he has everything arranged for the ceremony to take place here."

"Why does he set his heart on it? Perhaps I can persuade him to change his mind."

"Change my mind about what?" The Duke of Suffolk stood over her like some great eagle waiting to pounce.

"I cannot marry John!" she said fiercely. "I do not wish to be married."

"You have no say in the matter, my dear. You are but a child, and my ward. I can arrange a marriage for you if I so wish. It is the law."

"But what can you gain from it?" Margaret said in anguish. "I am just an ordinary lady of no great beauty or intelligence."

The Duke laughed cruelly. "You underestimate yourself, my dear Margaret. Don't you realise you are directly descended from King Edward the Third? Should our present King die with no heir, you would be in line for the throne."

"That is foolishness!" Margaret spoke hotly. "I have kinsmen; my uncle Edmund would be nearer than I."

"True enough," the Duke said, "but the Somerset family have a way of dying young, and I feel that your uncle, the Duke of Somerset, will be no exception. He is a hothead if ever I saw one."

"But even if that were the case," Margaret said firmly, "I am a mere woman and could never rule England."

Suffolk laughed. "My dear Margaret, that is where your husband would step in. At the worst we have nothing to lose; just think of the monies and estates you would bring John."

The Lady Alice swept into the hall tut-tutting and rubbing her hands impatiently.

"Do not stand there in the doorway. Come and be seated before the fire or you will catch your death of cold."

She smiled at Margaret and slipped her arm around her in a warm, friendly manner.

"I am delighted, child, that tomorrow you will wed my beloved John."

Tears blurred Margaret's vision as she stared into the bright logs burning in the enormous hearth. In the red flames she could see Edmund Tudor's burnished hair and she wondered sorrowfully if her hope of marriage to him was nothing more than a dream.

The Lady Alice had thought of everything. There was even a heavy cream gown, sewn with tiny pearls, for Margaret to wear at the wedding ceremony.

At her side stood John, silent and withdrawn, an unhappy expression on his handsome face. Even in her misery, Margaret could not bear to see him blame himself, and she reached out her hand towards him, resting it on his arm, trying to convey her understanding.

The Duke of Suffolk entered the chamber, in the company of a bishop resplendent in purple robes, and Margaret took a deep breath, fear making her tremble so much that John clasped her hand.

Outside the great hall, the storm burst forth in

all its fury, sending gales shrieking along the corridors and spitting darts of rain into the fire.

Margaret stood in numb resignation. There seemed no escape; nothing she could do to turn the tide of events. As the ceremony began, she was dimly aware of Lady Alice, dabbing at her eyes with a square of fine lace.

It seemed as if the ordeal lasted for hours. Margaret's head ached and her throat burned with unshed tears, but at last it was done and the Bishop nodded to the Duke.

The Lady Alice stepped forward and kissed her son warmly, and patted Margaret on the cheek.

"There, my sweet ones," she said effusively, "you are bound together in marriage. I am so happy for you."

The great hall with its high arched beams seemed to swing away in an arc over Margaret's head, and she sat down quickly, afraid that she was about to fall into a faint.

"Well, now, my dear Margaret, don't look so sorrowful. You could have made a worse match."

The Duke of Suffolk smiled down at her, eyes aglint with triumph.

"I see that you are well pleased, my lord," Margaret said hotly, "but the King will not take such a happening lightly, if I am any judge; and nor will his brothers Edmund and Jasper Tudor."

The Duke laughed. "Upstarts! That's all the

Tudors are, my dear. Descended from a Welsh bastard line. You are better without such people, take my word for it." He rested his hand on her shoulder in the familiar leering way that Margaret so hated. "I believe I have done both you and my son a favour by arranging your marriage."

She pulled away from him and began to walk; but he caught her arm so tightly that she winced with pain.

"I have not finished talking to you, my lady," he said severely. "I do not wish the marriage to be consummated as yet, the law does not allow it. But you must remember at all times that you are now married to a de la Pole, and act accordingly." He stared down at her. "There must be no more talk of an alliance with Edmund Tudor, do you understand?"

She stared at him defiantly and refused to answer. All she could feel was relief that her marriage with John was in name only for the present time.

The Duke smiled, as if reading her thoughts. "The time will quickly pass, my dear. You and John will come together soon enough."

He released her then and she turned and hurried out from the great hall, feeling the cold rush of the wind on her face drying her tears even as they fell.

"It is beyond all the bounds of reason!" Elizabeth's fingers trembled as she helped Margaret off with her shift. "How could the Duke dare to marry you to his son, without so much as a by-your-leave from the King?"

Margaret climbed into bed and lay down wearily, her eyes red and swollen from crying.

"Thanks be to all the saints that I was not old enough to take up residence with John de la Pole. I don't think I could have borne it if the Duke had forced me to stay away from the Court."

Elizabeth clucked her tongue in sympathy. "Just wait until my Lord of Richmond hears about this. He will not take the matter lightly. Nor will the King."

Margaret shook her head. "I don't know what can be done to alter events. It seems to me that I am wed for all of my life." She turned over wearily. "Please take the tapers away from the bedside, Elizabeth. The light hurts my eyes."

Elizabeth immediately smothered the flames.

"Try to sleep, Margaret," she advised. "In the morning you have an audience with the King."

Margaret shivered, wishing that Edmund was at Court so that he could help her and shelter her with his love, but he was away on the King's business and Margaret had never felt so alone in the whole of her young life.

"How dare Suffolk do such a thing to me?" The King was white with anger, his thin hands shaking as they plucked nervously at the fur of his robes. "Tell me again, my lady, was there an actual ceremony of marriage, or was it merely a betrothal between John de la Pole and yourself?"

Margaret's legs were cramped. She was in a curtsey, but the King had not thought to tell her to rise.

"It was a marriage, your Majesty," she said almost in a whisper. "A Bishop was present, I know that for sure."

The King strode across the chamber and behind him sat his French wife, her young face alive with curiosity. She looked down at Margaret with some amusement, wondering what the King would do to assert his authority.

"Rise child!" the King said impatiently. "And tell us how this situation was brought about."

Margaret glanced at the Queen. She was a good friend of Suffolk's, a fact well known to everyone except the King. She would no doubt supply him with full details of the meeting of which she was no more than an interested observer.

"I imagined I was about to make a simple visit, your Majesty," Margaret said uncertainly. "But when I arrived at the Duke's estate, everything was prepared; there was nothing I could do."

The King turned to her in a sudden burst of compassion. He rested his frail hand on her shoulder.

"My poor lady. If your father had lived, this would never have happened, but never fear, I will have the marriage annulled. It shall not stand as legal without the King's consent."

Suddenly the door of the chamber burst open and Edmund, Earl of Richmond, stood there, his colour high and his red-gold hair dishevelled. His eyes met Margaret's and she longed to rush into his arms, to feel his lips on hers.

He crossed the room and bowed to the King. "Sire, my chaplin came to tell me of your desire for my presence. He informed me of Suffolk's treasonable activities."

The Queen's eyebrows rose a fraction, but Edmund continued undeterred by her hard look.

"There was more behind this marriage than mere greed for a good arrangement for his son's future," he said quickly. "There is a great deal of unrest about the country and news has been brought to me that one of Suffolk's strongest followers, the Bishop of Chichester, has been caught and murdered."

Even the Queen paled and her hands shook a little as she turned to see the King's reaction. He rose from his chair and took Edmund's arm.

"Who has done this thing?" he asked nervously, his pale eyes filled with alarm.

"It was the sailors at Portsmouth, sire." Edmund took the King's arm, almost supporting him. "It seems that the Bishop offered them a portion of their pay instead of the whole and they were so incensed that they killed him."

Margaret made a quick prayer for the soul of the dead Bishop, though she could not see what bearing this terrible event could have on her own situation.

"Suffolk is to be brought against Parliament," Edmund went on. "The people have turned against him and there are certain charges he must answer."

The King put a hand over his face as if to shut out any unpleasantness. "I can't believe he would be guilty of any offense against my person," he said wearily.

Edmund stared uncomfortably at the Queen. Everyone knew that Suffolk had been instrumental in arranging the royal match and in so doing had made many concessions to Anjou that England could ill afford.

"Part of the deceit concerns the Lady Margaret," Edmund said. "He thought by marrying her to his son, he could take the throne from you, because of your lack of heirs."

The King was so pale that Margaret feared for his life. He stumbled a little as he walked to the door.

"I must pray and seek guidance," he said distractedly, and when his Queen rose with an impatient exclamation, he waved her aside.

Edmund took Margaret's arm and led her out of the chamber, and in spite of the distressing news he had brought the King, she was glowing with joy at his nearness.

"We will marry yet, Margaret," he said softly. "No one will be allowed to take you away from me."

She leaned against him, her heart filled with hope. If anything could be done, Edmund would be sure to see to it.

"What about the Duke?" she said, shuddering a little. As much as she disliked Suffolk, she would not like to see him suffer the same fate as the Bishop.

"He will be impeached, and will have to answer to Parliament and the King," he smiled. "But don't worry your soft heart, the most Henry will do is to exile the Duke. He is not a vindictive man, my brother the King."

He smiled down at her, his eyes shining. "You grow lovelier each time I see you. But you are so tiny. Are you never going to grow tall?"

Margaret blushed. "I am big enough to love you very dearly."

Her voice was little more than a whisper, but Edmund drew her close to him, briefly.

"Our marriage is written in the stars," he said softly. "We will have a fine son who will make his mark on England; I feel it deeply within me."

Edmund looked so sombre, and as the pale sun touched his hair, it was like a living flame. For a moment Margaret was frightened by the shadow that had come into his eyes, but then he smiled and it was gone.

"Come, don't be so serious," he said. "We are young and in love, and who knows what to-morrow might bring."

She curled her hand in his and as they walked through the long corridors together, she prayed that God and all the saints would look down and bless their union.

CHAPTER FIVE

"Oh, my lady, such terrible news!" Elizabeth stood in the doorway of Margaret's chamber nervously twisting her kerchief into little knots. "He's dead, Margaret. The Duke of Suffolk has been murdered!" She pushed the door, closing it with a bang, and came farther into the room.

Margaret, weak with shock, sank on to the bed, her wide eyes staring in disbelief.

"How could he be dead?" she said faintly. "I saw him take his leave of the King only a few days ago."

She could still see him, his face grown gaunt with the disgrace of his impeachment, stripped of his lands and honours. It had been as Edmund had said. The King had made the Duke an exile, though no one would have blamed his Majesty if he had sentenced the Duke to death.

"How did it happen?" Margaret asked, her lips dry as she thought of the Lady Alice and poor John de la Pole. How they must be suffering.

Elizabeth sat on a stool as if her legs had suddenly given way beneath her.

"It is so horrible a story, Margaret, I am half afraid to relate it." She stared down unseeingly at her twisted kerchief, her eyes dazed. "He put out to sea for his exile in France, but just off the coast there was a ship waiting for him. *Nicholas of the Tower*, it was. A royal ship. Though no one knows who sent her there."

She paused for a moment and Margaret wished she had the courage to tell Elizabeth to say no more, but somehow she was compelled to listen to the whole story.

"They took the Duke of Suffolk and put him on a small boat, my lady, and the lowest man of the crew, a lewd fellow it seems, was ordered to cut off the Duke's head."

Margaret drew a quick breath of horror and covered her mouth with her hand. Elizabeth stole a glance at her, anxious not to upset her more than was necessary.

"Was it quick and merciful, do you think?" Margaret said softly, and Elizabeth hesitated, knowing that soon the story would be all over the Court.

She shook her head. "No, it was not, my lady. A rusty blade was used to prolong the agony. And the sailors shouted that it was a fitting death for the traitor who would take the throne from the King."

Margaret rose and went to the window. She had been afraid of her guardian the Duke; she had almost hated him on times. But such a death was too awful for anyone to suffer.

She sighed. "I must visit his poor Duchess. She will need friends after this. Bring my jewel box, Elizabeth. I will take with me some gifts that the Lady Alice can turn into properties if she so wishes."

Margaret selected the ruby and gold collar

that had been her first gift from the Duke. She had never worn it since, but now at least it would serve some useful purpose.

"Do you think it wise to visit the Duchess at this time?" Elizabeth said cautiously. "The tide of opinion is turning against even her, and some are saying she may be impeached too."

"It may not be wise," Margaret said firmly, "but I must go all the same. She offered me nothing but kindness when I was under her roof."

"Then let me bring Edmund, Earl of Richmond, to you," Elizabeth persuaded. "You are too young to wander abroad alone."

Margaret nodded. "Yes, he will take me. That's an excellent idea, Elizabeth. Go now, and by the time you return I will be ready."

Edmund was reluctant to allow Margaret to make the journey. He came to her chamber quickly, his face drawn and anxious.

"Margaret." He took her hands in his, kissing the tips of her fingers. "You do not realise what dangers you face by visiting the Duchess. The people are in an ugly mood and will not stop to think of stoning anyone who so much as stops outside Suffolk's home."

Margaret regarded him steadily. "I'm sure you will find a way Edmund. I must go to see her. Please."

He could not resist the pleading in her eyes. He shrugged his shoulders and drew her to the door.

"Very well, Margaret. But you must not stay long. Do you understand?"

His words were softened by the smile he gave her and Margaret's heart missed a beat. She loved him so much it was almost like a pain inside her.

She stood on tiptoe and briefly pressed her lips to his. "I understand, Edmund," she said softly.

Heavy drapes shut out the smallest vestige of sunlight and the atmosphere was heavy with the scent of lavender water. Margaret stood over the bed and looked with pity at the pallid shrunken face of the Duchess of Suffolk.

"My Lady Alice," she said softly. "I have brought some small gifts for you."

The Duchess opened her eyes so slowly it was as if her lids were weighted with the burden of her grief.

"Margaret, is that you, child? Ah, if only you were old enough to be John's bride in deed, I would be happy about his future." She held up a thin white hand that shook as Margaret touched it.

"I'm sorry," Margaret whispered. "Is there anything I can do?"

The Duchess shook her head wearily, the grey curls escaping from her cap in thin, unsightly wisps. "No one can help me now. My lord has been cruelly taken from me. All I wish now is to be with him."

Compassion burned inside Margaret. She

leaned over the Duchess and smoothed back her hair.

"You have your son John, and he needs you more than ever now. Try to become well again, for his sake."

Wearily Alice turned away. "I will try, my dear Margaret, but I fear all the spirit has gone from me with the death of my lord."

As Margaret left the darkened chamber, there were tears on her cheeks. She felt heavy-hearted so that even Edmund's comforting arm could not lift the gloom that had settled upon hers.

"I should not have allowed you to come!" Edmund said. "And if you do not try to smile, I shall feel guilty for ever more."

Margaret laid her head on his shoulder, and tried to stop the tears that fell so swiftly along her smooth cheeks.

"I cry not so much for the Lady Alice," she said softly, "but I am thinking of how I would feel if you should be taken from me."

Edmund shivered suddenly and for a moment was silent; then he held her close, his lips against her hair.

"I will always be with you," he said softly.

The King would speak to no one. He roamed about his rooms like a restless spirit, neither eating nor sleeping, and it was whispered around the Court that Henry the Sixth of England was almost mad from grief and guilt at the death of his chief minister.

In solemn dignity, Suffolk's mutilated body had been brought from the shores of Kent to be given a decent burial. And now the King had hidden himself away, and not even his vivacious Queen could bring him out of his misery.

Margaret, feeling the same sadness that had settled over the rest of the court, dressed soberly, decorating her dark gown only with the thinnest gold collars. The idea took fire, and soon the other ladies were attempting to outdo each other in modesty of dress, and soon it seemed as if the whole Court was in mourning.

"Things are going to get worse before they get better," Elizabeth said dolefully. "You mark my words, the country is in an awful state!"

Margaret looked at her, alarmed. "What do you mean? Your words sound so distressing."

"I only speak the truth." Elizabeth shook out a jewel-bright gown, folding it neatly away with lavender slipped into the folds to keep it sweet. "The common people are up in arms. They are afraid of the weakness of the King and the way the barons are gaining power."

Both Margaret and Elizabeth jumped nervously as someone rapped loudly on the door. After a moment's hesitation, Elizabeth flung it open. Edmund hurried towards them and took Margaret into his arms, and she breathed in the fresh, wind-blown scent of him with delight.

"You must leave here immediately," he said quickly. "A fellow by the name of Jack Cade is gathering men to march on London."

Edmund stopped for breath and Margaret clung to him, suddenly afraid.

"I want to be with you," she said. "Edmund, please let me stay with you."

He shook his head. "This Jack Cade has already routed the Staffords at Sevenoaks, and I must help the King withdraw to Coventry where he will be safe." He kissed her swiftly. "Prepare to join the rest of the ladies in the great hall. You will be taken out of town until the danger is past." He released her and Margaret felt her heart leave her body.

"Oh, Edmund, what if I should never see you again?"

She pressed her hand to her lips and stifled a cry. Edmund stood for a moment, his eyes regarding her steadily.

"I will be with you again, I promise you. Now try to be brave for all our sakes." He smiled quickly. "Haven't I promised that we will have a son? Don't worry. It is not my time to die."

Before she could answer him, he had swung out of the door and as his footsteps died away in the distance, Margaret felt some of his courage fire her blood.

The King's retinue was already leaving. Outside on the green, horses stamped impatiently, lifting their heads to the scented air, nostrils flaring.

Margaret stood on a box to get a better view, trying desperately to see Edmund, but under the glinting helmets and fluttering banners, all men looked the same.

"Come, Margaret," Elizabeth returned to the room, the ribbons from her head-dress flying. "We must join the other ladies in the great hall." She rummaged into a chest, drawing out a thick woollen cloak. "Put this on. You will, no doubt, need it before our journey is over."

Margaret turned from the window with a sigh and in spite of her fear for Edmund, her heart was stirred to pride at the noble sight of the King and his men riding off into the distance.

Elizabeth pulled the cloak around Margaret's shoulders, her face pale.

"The ladies are acting like a lot of foolish geese!" she said disapprovingly. "Some of them are screaming and giving way to the vapours as if they are about to be ravished on the spot. We have plenty of time if we keep our heads."

Margaret attempted a smile. "We will show them how to behave with dignity," she said, and pulled at the door. It resisted her efforts and she tugged harder, an expression of concern on her face. "Elizabeth, help me. The door seems to be stuck fast."

With growing fear, they both pulled at the heavy door, but it would not move.

Elizabeth hurried to the window. "They are leaving, Margaret, all the ladies are leaving. We'll be here alone!"

Margaret climbed on to the box in front of the window and leaned out as far as she dared.

"Hand me some linen cloth that I can wave to

attract attention," she said urgently and quickly.

Elizabeth obeyed.

"It's no good!" Margaret leaned against the sill, her arm aching and her throat dry. "My shouts are drowned by the noise of the horses. They will never hear us now."

Soon the courtyard was empty except for a few hens scratching in the dust.

"What shall we do?"

Elizabeth looked to Margaret for direction, forgetting that she was a young girl, seeing only the firm chin and steady eyes and the firmness of the small hands clasped together as if in prayer.

"We are not all that high up," Margaret said at last. "I think if we hold on to the vines and climb down, from window to window, we should be quite safe."

"But Margaret, the vines might break!" Elizabeth seemed horrified, her eyes large in her pale face.

"The alternative is to stay here and be ravished! Is that more to your liking?" Margaret said with a smile. She moved over to the chest and pulled out a dark gown and a cloak. "We must dress as plainly as possible," she said reasonably, "otherwise we may be set upon and robbed. Come along, Elizabeth. No good can be done by just sitting here."

Margaret climbed on to the sill and, leaning precariously out of the window, caught at one of the thick vines that grew in a profusion over the castle walls.

"I'll go first, and you can see how I find footholds," she said, excitement lending fresh colour to her face.

She swung out over the window ledge, filled with a sensation of breathlessness as for a moment she was suspended high above the ground. Then the rough of the stonework was scraping her knees before her feet found crevices on which to balance herself.

Inch by inch, she lowered herself on aching arms, fearing at any moment the vines would give way from the wall and send her hurtling into the cobbled yard.

"Come along, Elizabeth!" She managed to put some assurance into her voice. "It is almost as easy as walking down the stairs!"

Above her, Elizabeth gave a little cry as a bird's nest came away in her hand, scattering dried mud and twigs over Margaret's head.

"Don't worry, Elizabeth, the birds can fly. We cannot, so keep going."

It seemed as if they were climbing for hours, but at last Margaret felt the firm ground beneath her feet. She held her arms up to encourage Elizabeth who was still far above.

"There, you see, Elizabeth, it can be done! You are nearly on the ground; just a little more effort."

At last, Elizabeth sat panting on the cold cobbles, her hands red and scratched and a smear of mud over her eyebrow. Margaret leaned back against the wall and laughed until the tears flowed down her cheeks.

Elizabeth, after a moment, began to laugh too, rubbing her hands against the dark cloak, staining it with mud.

"I do believe you are enjoying the situation, Margaret," she accused, her eyes bright though her tone was reproving. "If your mother, the Duchess of Somerset, could see you now, I really don't know what she'd say."

Margaret scrambled to her feet. "I don't think we should stay here wasting our time in speculation," she laughed. "We've got a long way to go, and we'd better start walking."

She pulled her cloak more closely around her and threaded her arm through Elizabeth's.

"Come along, there is no need for misery. Think of this as adventure," she said cheerily and Elizabeth laughed.

"My Lord Edmund, Earl of Richmond, will not think of it as an adventure. He will, no doubt, have a blue fit when he finds out about it!"

Margaret smiled impishly, her hair tossed by the wind and the rich colour flooding her face and at that moment, Elizabeth saw that child that Margaret was never allowed to be.

The streets of London were ominously quiet. Occasionally, a child cried or a dog barked, only to be swiftly hushed behind closed windows and bolted doors.

"I have never seen the place like this," Margaret exclaimed. "Everything so dead and eerie. I would swear it was a different London to that I have always seen, with banners floating from windows and the people thronging the road-side."

"These are strange times," Elizabeth said gloomily. "We're likely to be set upon by cut-throats if we don't find our way to my uncle's house soon."

"You think he will welcome us?" Margaret asked anxiously. "Perhaps he will lend us a horse and some money so that I can return to Bletsoe."

She was growing tired now. They had walked a long way and her shoes had never been made for tramping along dusty cobbled streets. But for Elizabeth's sake, she tried to remain cheerful.

Suddenly, from the direction of London Bridge, came a loud roaring noise that had almost an animal quality about it. Elizabeth stopped in fright, and Margaret turned back to her.

The streets were thick with people, running and pushing, crying out in hoarse voices.

"What is it?" Margaret said in sudden alarm. "What has happened?"

As if in answer to her question, a man at her side shouted out in fury. "They have killed Lord Say! And the Sheriff of Kent has died too at the hands of the rebels. Are we going to stop these ruffians before they over-run our homes?"

A great cheer went up and the crowd surged forward. Elizabeth pulled at Margaret's cloak.

"Quick, into this doorway, or you will be trampled under foot."

They pressed in terror against the rough wood, while the shouting mass of people streamed past them and Margaret pressed her hands over her ears to shut out the ragged chant that rose like a wave over the frenzied people.

"Kill Cade! Kill Cade! Jack Cade must die!"

Suddenly a door near them was thrust open and a hand beckoned them inside. Elizabeth nodded to Margaret. Anything was preferable to standing unprotected in the street.

"You will be safe in here," said a voice from the dimness, and then thankfully the noise of the crowd was shut out.

As Margaret's eyes became accustomed to the gloom, she saw an old lady indicating that they follow her into a back room. It was small and ill-lit, but clean and smelling sweetly of herbs.

"I knew you would come to me today, Margaret Beaufort." The woman smiled, rubbing her old hands against the crisp white of her apron. "My house is honoured to receive you. Please be seated. I have a message for you."

Margaret sank into a chair, her legs trembling. Suddenly the years of knowledge in the old lady's strange eyes was more frightening than anything she had experienced on this strangest of days.

"How could you know I'd be here when this morning I didn't even know it myself?" she said shakily.

The woman shrugged her bony shoulders. "There are some who call me witch," she said gently, "but I mean no harm. I have a message to deliver to you and then I will help you to get away from here. Everything is taken care of."

Margaret stared at her. "You were so sure we would be here then?"

The woman nodded. "My voices never lie to me, my lady. I knew you would come. I even knew the time and saw you crouched against the door in a stained woollen cloak."

Margaret pressed her hands together to stop them from shaking. She longed to touch the cross at her throat for comfort, but she was not sure that it would be the most tactful thing to do at the moment.

"My message is brief," the woman said softly, "but drink some of my home-made wine; it will bring colour once more into your cheeks."

She smiled so kindly that Margaret smiled too, and took the cup that was offered.

"Many thanks for your hospitality. I hope some day I shall be able to repay you."

The woman shook her head gently. "I think not, my lady. Once I have seen you, my purpose here is done. But no matter. Let me tell you what I have seen." She leaned forward urgently. "You are to marry a man with hair the colour of flame, and between you will bring forth the King of England." She paused for a moment. "Marry no other than Edmund of Richmond; he is the chosen husband for you."

Margaret stared in surprise. "But how could you know all this?" she said quickly. "And anyway, there is no way that a son of mine could be King of England. There are too many heirs alive and well. It just could not be."

The woman smiled. "You will see my words come true one day, but not before you have known great grief."

She rose to her feet and such was her presence that Margaret rose too.

Suddenly she felt quite weak and ill. Her head ached, her feet were sore, and her legs stung as if a thousand wasps were busy about them.

She turned to speak to Elizabeth, but she was standing at the small window.

"The Kentish men are retreating over the bridge!" she said excitedly. "The Londoners have won!"

Margaret was so weary that she lay her head back against the dark wall and closed her eyes and the room swam in tiny circles around her head.

Margaret awakened to find Edmund leaning over her, his bright hair falling over his forehead in the way that she loved. She reached up a hand and he caught it, trapping it between his fingers.

"You are safe now," he smiled down at her, "though when I heard what had happened, my heart nearly stopped beating. There. Is it not beating unevenly at this moment?" He pressed his lips on hers and she clung to him.

"Where am I, Edmund? What has happened?" She struggled to sit up, but he restrained her.

"You are at the house of Elizabeth's uncle, if you must know." He smiled to soften his words. "And quite a lot has happened; but first the King is safe. Jasper remains with him." He smoothed her arm. "Cade was captured and his head adorns London Bridge — a fitting end for a rebel."

Margaret shuddered, remembering again the noise of the crowd. Edmund pressed her close to him.

"The sooner we are married, the better! Then I can keep you out of trouble!"

He laughed and pinched her cheek. She closed her eyes, wondering what he would say if she told him of the old woman's prophecy, that she would one day bear his son, a son who would grow up to be the King of England.

"Why the secret smile?" he asked, looking down at her indulgently.

"Perhaps some day I'll tell you," she said, and burrowed her face happily against his shoulder.

CHAPTER SIX

The court seemed to take on new life. Ladies huddled in little knots like posies of flowers, their gay dresses bringing splashes of colour to the great hall. And down in the kitchens, the cooks worked in the heat that shimmered from the roasting spits, filling the ovens to capacity with brown crusted pies.

The King sat often listening to the musicians, a happy if somewhat vague smile on his pale face, while his Queen walked the corridors with a new dignity because she was with child.

She was not inclined to quarrel now with the great lords, haranguing them about the state of the country; instead she took up her embroidery frame, working the colours with womanly patience that was becoming to her state.

Margaret could not help but envy her. "She looks so proud," she told Elizabeth. "She has even removed her girdle of rich gems so that her condition can be seen more easily."

Elizabeth looked up with shrewd eyes. "And I wonder who the father is? Not the King, I'll warrant!"

Margaret looked round quickly, fearful that someone might hear.

"Hush, it's treason you speak. Someone will carry tales to the Queen, and then where will you be?"

"I speak truth," Elizabeth said firmly. "The Frenchwoman has lain with more English lords than she care tell about. Why, she has even shared the bed of Jasper Tudor, for all he is half-brother to the King."

"You have not seen this with your own eyes, Elizabeth, and I would prefer you not to speak about the matter any more. The King seems happier than he's been for a long time." She sighed, quickly changing the subject. "I wonder if I will ever be wife to Edmund? For all I know, I am still joined in marriage to John de la Pole."

Margaret looked through the window at the rolling fields, her eyes thoughtful.

"The King has not mentioned my marriage to Edmund since the death of the Duke of Suffolk. I wish he would make up his mind to speak and put me out of my misery."

Elizabeth nodded her head shrewdly. "Edmund, Earl of Richmond, will bring matters to a head quite soon! He is an impatient man and I can tell by the look in his eyes when they rest upon you that he won't delay much longer."

Margaret felt the warm colour suffuse her cheeks. She too had seen the look in Edmund's eyes, and it had the power to make her heart beat faster.

She went and stood before her mirror, seeing with delight the new angles that added maturity to her face now that the plumpness of childhood had left it. She was small-framed, it was true, but her breasts curved gently under the rich velvet of

78

her gown and her waist was so tiny that the girdle of gold and precious stones hung loosely around the soft curve of her hips.

She smiled, wondering how she appeared in Edmund's eyes. She hoped with all her heart that he found her desirable and womanly.

It was a pale, misty evening when the King at last sent a command that she appear before him.

"Come quickly," Elizabeth fluttered round her in a panic. "You must let me help you with your gown. The King must see how lovely you can look."

Margaret smiled serenely, though deep inside it seemed she had a dozen butterflies fluttering their wings.

"I'll wear the blue velvet," she said, her voice surprisingly firm. "And the collar and girdle of matching silver and gold. I do not wish to make Edmund ashamed of his choice."

As she entered the royal chamber, Margaret saw the King sitting straight in his chair. His eyes were bright and he seemed well and in good spirits.

Edmund came to her and took her hand in his, leading her towards the King. He bowed, smiling affectionately.

"Henry," he said warmly, "it is good to see you looking so well."

He straightened then and addressed his brother formally.

"Sire, in the light of the recent impeachment of the Duke of Suffolk, I have come to ask that the wardship of Margaret Beaufort, heiress of John, first Duke of Somerset, should be given into the keeping of myself and my brother Jasper Tudor, jointly."

He smiled down at Margaret, warm and re-assuring.

"And more, your Majesty. I seek your permission to marry the Lady Margaret as indeed was your own wish."

The King smiled, though there were deep shadows under his eyes and lines of strain etched heavy around his mouth.

"I grant both requests most happily," he said. "The marriage of Margaret to John de la Pole is null and void because of Suffolk's treasonable acts. It must be removed from all records, as if it had never been." He smiled at them both. "God go with you, and may your union prove happy and fruitful."

The Queen, coming to his side, smiled, happy in her own proven fruitfulness, and for the first time Margaret realised there was a soft side to the King's wife.

Outside in the long cool corridor, Edmund took Margaret gently in his arms and kissed her.

"We can thank the saints that the King was in his right senses," he said, "today he was almost his old self."

Smiling, he took her hand in his and she leaned against him, enjoying the warmth of his closeness. He was all she would ever ask in a husband.

Hands touching and heads bent toward each other, they moved happily along the dark tunnel of the corridor.

Margaret saw the old familiar walls of her home at Bletsoe, mellow in the early sunlight, and realised with a pang how much she had missed its gracious silence.

It seemed a lifetime ago since the Duke of Suffolk had come to take her away to the busy liveliness of the Court.

Her mother appeared at an upper window, waving a bright scarf, and Margaret smiled, guessing that the retinue from the King's own bodyguard had been spotted from miles away, and that the Duchess had been waiting in a fever of impatience for several hours.

"There!" she said laughingly to Edmund. "My mother, the Duchess of Somerset, is not such a dragon, is she?"

Edmund inclined his head, his eyes bright with amusement, and gave Margaret a quick look.

"Indeed she is not a dragon, I think I may even prefer the mother to the daughter!"

Margaret tossed her head, pretending to be insulted, and Edmund threw back his head, laughing in delight.

Lionel, Lord Welles, was waiting to welcome them. He drew them into the great hall with its cheerful fire of logs and filled goblets with sparkling wine.

"It is good to see you home, Margaret."

He put his arm around her shoulder and kissed her cheek and she embraced him, remembering with a surge of tears how kind he'd been to her when she was a child. Some had said he was thinking of the vast fortune that came with the widowed Duchess of Somerset and her young daughter, but Margaret had always known that the match was truly one of love.

"It is wonderful to be here, Lionel, and I do believe you are more handsome than ever."

She spoke with sincerity. His hair stood up dark and crisp and his cheeks had the colour of the outdoors, so that he looked younger than his years.

The Duchess swept into the room. Her cheeks were warm, and it was obvious that she had hurried down to welcome them.

"Oh, Margaret, you are so much grown that I hardly know you." She kissed her daughter decorously and she still possessed the dignity and poise that Margaret had always envied. "Come, we will eat. You must be tired and hungry."

She smiled at Edmund, and he bowed quickly over her hand.

"You are as lovely as your daughter," he said, and the surprised Duchess blushed with pleasure.

When they were settled at the table, Margaret glanced at Edmund from under her lashes. He was deep in conversation with Lionel and was as much at home here as in the Court of the King.

She felt full of pride because this handsome, charming man loved her and wished to marry her.

Edmund turned to her suddenly. "What are you dreaming about?" he whispered, and touched her hand beneath the table.

She smiled up at him, feeling absurdly shy with her mother present. "Only how well you fit in with any surroundings," she said softly.

Her mother leaned forward. "Have some peacock breast. Or if that is not to your fancy, we have heron in verjuice and wine, cooked specially for your arrival."

The atmosphere at table was genial and when the enormous meal was finished, Margaret rose and went with her mother to her old chambers.

"You see, Margaret, I have kept your room just as you left it." She leaned forward to touch a brilliant tapestry on the wall. "This is the very first of your carpets. I keep it proudly. You were always good with your needle."

Margaret smiled happily, pleased with the compliment. It seemed that she would have much more in common with her mother now than she ever had as a child.

As if to confirm her judgment, the Duchess sat on the edge of the bed in an attitude of complete informality.

"Come, now, tell me your news," she said softly. "Is the wedding to be soon?" Without waiting for an answer, she hurried on. "And what of the Queen? Can it be true that she is with child? And the King — there is talk he has not been himself since Suffolk's death. Come, child, tell me everything that has been happening at Court!"

Margaret smiled and obediently sat on the small stool and folded her hands together.

"I'm quite willing to tell you, mother," she said happily, "but there is so much it is difficult to know where to start."

It was strange to be sitting back in her old room at Bletsoe, Margaret reflected when at last her mother had gone. She went to the window and looked out at the darkening overcast skies, and shivered a little. Still, tomorrow would be fine and then she and Edmund could ride out together.

Soon she would go with him to his native Wales, and she would love it because it was the country that had bred him; but first she would teach Edmund to love the quiet fields of Bedfordshire.

The days passed in a succession of happy events that seemed to stand out in Margaret's mind like a bright pattern of shapes and colours. The lush green of the sunlit fields, the red-gold of Edmund's hair, and the jewel shades of dresses and doublets against the grey mellow walls of Bletsoe.

It was as if all her senses were heightened towards a shining peak of happiness that ran like a gold thread through all the carefree days.

It was to end more abruptly than she'd antici-pated. The dew of an early summer's morning was still on the grass when a rider came galloping at full speed up to the great doors of the house. Edmund was to return to Court at once. The King had been victim to some kind of seizure, and was gravely ill.

Preparations were made to begin the journey at once and as Margaret rode away from the walls of her home for the second time, it seemed that once again she was making a journey into the unknown.

Elizabeth wrung out a square of linen into a bowl of scented water and dabbed Margaret's red-rimmed eyes gently.

"Come now, Margaret," she said, "there is no need to weep for the King. He is quite unaware of your tears."

"But if you could see him, Elizabeth." Mar-garet could scarcely bring herself to speak about it. "He raves and staggers around his chamber until he falls into a deathly silence, not speaking or moving. It is pitiful."

Elizabeth handed a partly sewn tapestry to Margaret and smiled encouragingly.

"Try some new patterns. It may take your mind off the King's illness."

Margaret looked down at the bright silk threads, her face white and drawn.

"Some are saying that the King is tainted with madness from his grandfather, the King of

France. He spent his last days completely devoid of his senses."

Margaret shuddered even as she spoke the words aloud. Her own Edmund was descended from Charles of France through his mother, Queen Catherine. Was it possible that he too could inherit such dread illness of the mind?

"Oh, Elizabeth, could Edmund fall sick in this way, do you think?" she said faintly.

"Not him!" Elizabeth spoke with certainty. "He is descended on his father's side from tough Welsh stock. Why, you've only to look at him to see there is no weakness in him."

Margaret was comforted. There was a great deal of sense in what Elizabeth said, and why go out to look for trouble when there was trouble a-plenty on the doorstep?

Even now, Richard of York was trying to influence Parliament to make him the King's protector. That would put her uncle, the Duke of Somerset, in an invidious position. It could even mean that Edmund and Jasper Tudor be banished from the Court, and the thought made her feel physically sick.

Richard was descended from the same royal line as she herself and he did not seem an evil or over-ambitious man, but when there was a crown at stake it was hard to tell how anyone would act.

She picked up her needle. Elizabeth was right. The best thing to do would be to free her mind of all morbid fears; no good would come of worrying. And yet even as the resolution was made, her needle became idle and there was a worried frown between her eyes.

The corridors were busy with women carrying white linen and a strange mixture of bowls and jars. They scurried to and fro like busy ants, skirts swishing and veils flying.

In the Queen's chamber, tapers had been placed close together to provide more light.

On the great bed, the Queen of England lay tossing in silent agony, her hands gripping the sheets so that the material was strained to breaking point.

It was almost time for the King's heir to be born.

Margaret took her place with the other ladies around the bed, helping as best she could by placing a scented cloth on the Queen's hot brow. She knew a deep pity as she saw the dry lips move. The Queen was saying her prayers, no doubt in her native French.

Margaret was amazed by the way she bit with small white teeth into her lip, drawing blood, retaining her dignity at all costs.

At last, with a strangled gasp, the young Queen gave birth to her child and lay for a moment exhausted against the bolster.

The physician came forward proudly. "It is a son, madam," he said loftily as if he had done the whole thing alone.

"His name will be Edward," the Queen said

imperiously, her delight at the birth of a male heir conquering her weariness. "My Lord Duke of Buckingham, please to take the prince to his father so that the King may rejoice in his son."

Margaret went along the corridor behind the Duke of Buckingham who gingerly carried the tiny Prince of Wales on a soft cushion in his arms. Guards fell away from the door of the royal chamber like leaves in the wind and Buckingham went forward purposefully.

The King sat like an urchin on the ground, his pale eyes gazing at something only he could see. His hair was unkempt and fell in wisps over his face, and his thin hands plucked nervously at the folds of his robes.

Buckingham coughed. "Your Majesty, I bring your son and heir, Edward, Prince of Wales."

There was no response from the King, not the slightest sign that he'd understood or even heard what was said.

Edmund Tudor took the King's arm. "Come and sit upon your throne, Henry," he said softly, as though to a child. "Let me place your crown upon your head. You are the King of England, remember?"

The King looked into Edmund's eyes for a moment with almost a lucid expression, but then his head drooped and the crown rolled across the chamber.

In the silence, Buckingham tried manfully to attract the King's attention. "Sire, behold your son and heir," he said almost desperately. But with a fretful cry, Henry turned his face to the blank wall again.

At last, Edmund drew Buckingham away. "Come, my lord," he said softly. "Perhaps time can achieve what a son cannot."

They withdrew, bowing with respect, even though Henry stared away from them, unaware of their existence.

"York will demand to be made protector of the small prince. It is inevitable," Buckingham said sadly. "And who is going to break the news to the Queen that her husband does not recognise their own son?"

"I will do it," Edmund said quickly. "The Queen can accuse me of nothing, for the King is my own flesh and blood, after all."

Margaret of Anjou lay still in her childbed. She had more colour now and her eyes were bright with a fierce motherlove as they rested on the baby Buckingham returned to her arms.

From the back of the crowd, Margaret stood, feeling ill and unhappy; seeing the King like that had left her feeling weak and upset. But she watched with pride as Edmund went and bowed over the Queen's hand.

"Madam, the King does not respond when we speak to him. He sees nothing. Not even his own son."

The Queen held her hand out in supplication to Edmund. "What will become of us if the King does not recover?" she said in a whisper.

"Do not be afraid," Edmund spoke kindly.

"Even if Richard of York becomes protector, he will have regard for your son's position. He would not dream of doing him harm."

Margaret stared at him fiercely. "Harm? Oh, no, he will not pierce him with a sword, but he will steal what is rightfully the King's, for all that, and when my son grows up there will be nothing for him."

She began to weep and waved her hand to her ladies impatiently; they clustered round her anxiously.

"Send to the Pope. He must say a special Mass for the King's swift return to health."

Margaret met Edmund's eyes and she knew his thoughts were the same as hers. Admiration for the young Queen, who would not admit defeat even though it was staring her in the face.

Silently they made their way from the chamber and out into the corridor, their hands meeting in a silent message of hope and love.

CHAPTER SEVEN

Margaret's cream satin dress hung in heavy folds to her small feet. Rich pearls added a warmth and lustre to the cloth that was duplicated in the fine white veil on her hair.

At her side stood Edmund, Earl of Richmond, a man full grown with twenty-five years resting lightly on his broad shoulders. His burnished hair setting him apart from other men.

The Bishop lifted his hand in blessing and Margaret realised that the ceremony was over. She was Edmund's bride and nothing could part them, except death itself.

Elizabeth was the first to step forward and kiss her cheek, and there were tears in her eyes.

"How lovely you look," she said with emotion. "And so young and slender — just thirteen years old. Why, it seems only the other day that I brought you from Bletsoe to be at the Court."

No one spoke of Suffolk who had dominated her life and held a hasty ceremony of marriage between Margaret and John de la Pole. Margaret shuddered. That was all in the past! Suffolk was dead and Edmund, her dear husband, held her well-being in his capable hands.

The King came forward and took her hand. He was so much better, that Margaret smiled happily at him, forgetting for the moment that he was monarch and thinking only of him as kin to her dear husband.

But life at Court had not been without its anxious moments. For a time, Richard of York had been protector to the Prince of Wales; and Somerset, Margaret's uncle, had been thrown into prison. She had feared for his life then, but all thanks to the saints, the King had recovered and the old order of things had been restored.

"May you have a long life together and many sons!" The King put an affectionate arm around his brother's shoulder. He loved Edmund well and had heaped honours upon him so that now he was premier earl in all the kingdom.

"The bedding ceremony!" a voice cried. "Let it begin."

There was a murmur from the ladies present and the hot colour rose to Margaret's cheeks. She stood hesitating for a moment, looking toward her new husband, as if for guidance. He smiled his encouragement, and she suffered her ladies to lead her away.

In the flower-decked chamber, Elizabeth was already busy sprinkling herbs over the bed-covers.

"This will ensure fertility, Margaret," she smiled mischievously. "Though I doubt you will need it with a man like Edmund Tudor for a husband!"

She kissed Margaret's cheek soundly. "The Earl is a real man, one whom any woman would be proud to bed with. Just leave yourself in his hands. He will care for you with kindness and love."

She untied the ribbons on Margaret's gown and it fell in heavy folds to lie like snow against the floor. Her hair was undone, and it hung in soft curls to her waist.

"You are lovely and innocent as a child," Edmund said, his eyes alight with love. "And more beautiful than even I expected."

Margaret stared at him shyly. He looked unfamiliar in a loose robe of emerald green. She clung to his hand, afraid that in her inexperience she would fail him. He must have read a little of her thoughts in her eyes.

"Don't be afraid, Margaret; you will be happy with me, I promise you."

At last the moment came for the giggling ladies to leave the chamber. Edmund secured the door and then slowly came towards her. Margaret began to tremble. She wanted to be in his arms, to become truly his wife, and yet something within her was shrinking from the new experience that would change her from a virgin girl into a woman.

Edmund swept her up and laid her gently on the bed, his hands warm, gently caressing her. She felt his mouth possessing hers and love blossomed within her like an opening flower. She clung to him, delighting in his passion for her, determined to be a good and faithful wife for as long as they both should live.

"Marriage agrees with you, my lady." Elizabeth carried the tapestries out into the green garden, handing Margaret several brightly coloured strands of silk.

"I know it does." Margaret laughed out loud, happiness soaring through her like a bird flying up to the endless sky. "I am more than fortunate to have found such a wonderful love so early in life, and I thank Saint Nicholas every day for guiding me to Edmund."

She used her needle delicately, fashioning a rose of pale beauty into the design of the carpet.

Elizabeth sighed. "I wish I had your hand with a needle. My roses all look like drooping butterflies."

Margaret laughed once more; joy came easy to her these days. She rested her tapestry against her skirt.

"Oh, if only Edmund could remain at my side all day as well as all night, how wonderful it would be."

Elizabeth nodded wisely. "There would be no tapestry work done then, and you would be exhausted with enjoyment of your husband!"

The ready colour suffused Margaret's cheeks. "Shame on you, Elizabeth, that you, an unmarried lady, should talk so!"

"I am twice your age, my dear Margaret, and not come to that without tasting of forbidden fruits." She laughed. "And there is no need for you to look so shocked. You wouldn't have me a dried-up, loveless maid now, would you?"

Margaret suppressed a giggle and bent once more over her needlework.

"I shall have many fine sons for Edmund's sake. His own mother bore four boys and two girls, so I have something to live up to."

Elizabeth frowned. "You would not like six children, Margaret? Queen Catherine did not live to enjoy her brood, remember?"

"Well, the Queen was too old for child-bearing. I shall have my sons while I am young and strong, you'll see."

Margaret lifted her face to the sun, happiness flowing from her like a perfume.

Surreptitiously, Elizabeth made the sign of the cross. It did not do to call the attention of the saints to oneself the way Margaret was doing. But then she was young and the young always imagine that their life will always be a bed of roses.

The sound of horses in the courtyard brought Margaret to her feet.

"Edmund is home!" she cried, and lifting her skirts like a child, ran across the green to meet him.

Laughing, he lifted her high into the air and she hung like a tiny doll waiting for him to set her down. "Look who has come to see you. Some fine visitors. Are you not going to speak words of welcome, my lady?"

Margaret was aware of Edmund's teasing, and blushed crimson, conscious of her crumpled blue dress and of the tendrils of hair escaping around her neck.

One man stepped forward to bend over her

hand with an amused smile, and she almost revealed her surprise to see that it was the Duke of York.

"I am truly honoured, dear Margaret. I had not realised what a beauty you had become."

Margaret dipped before him politely, feeling tongue-tied and uncertain before this man who was reputed to be an enemy of the King.

Edmund saw her confusion, and ushering the guests towards their chambers, he turned for a moment to whisper to her.

"This is a business meeting, my love, it will soon be over."

"They are all kinsmen to us and to each other!" Margaret studied the guests as they sat themselves comfortably around the large room.

Edmund smiled and nodded. "That is just the point, Margaret. This business concerns all of us."

Lord Powys bent his tall figure down to kiss Margaret's hand and smiled a little at her shyness. His large friendly eyes lit up to see the colour rise to her cheeks.

Edmund raised his cup and made a toast — "Kirkstall Abbey!" He held out his hand to Margaret and she sat at his side more than a little relieved to be out of the limelight.

"I think we are all agreed on this issue," Edmund said clearly, "as joint heirs to the Earl of Kent, we are each entitled to £90 out of the property of Kirkstall Abbey." He drank from his cup before continuing. "The manor has greatly decreased in value, and so to make it easier for Abbot William, we propose to petition the King to lower our dues to £75, I think that should help."

Richard of York rose to his feet, his eyes bright with good humour. "Are we all agreed on it, gentlemen?" he said, and amongst a murmur of assent, he turned to Margaret holding out his cup.

Quickly she gave him more of the ruby wine, shaking a little in her nervousness of him. He smiled and took her hand in his.

"Please, my lady, I am not a dragon. Such a pretty young lady should be afraid of no man."

She backed away from him, feeling foolish as the rest of the gathering burst into laughter. Edmund took her hand firmly in his and she clung to him, grateful for his nearness.

"The Lady Margaret may be the youngest one among us," he said mildly, "but she has just as big a share in the manor of Kirkstall Abbey, and she is generous to a fault. I know she would take nothing from Abbot William if she thought she could help him even further."

Richard of York bowed and his eyes were mocking. "How wonderful to see a love-match in these days of convenient marriages. I am quite envious, Edmund."

Margaret stole a look at him from under her lashes and saw that he did indeed look sincere in his protestations. She felt just a little sorry for him, though even now he was attempting to become protector to the little Prince Edward.

At last, the guests took their leave, and Margaret sank down against the cushions, her head aching.

Edmund came to her and took her in his arms very gently, his eyes dark and mysterious with the passion that was always very near the surface.

"Do not send for your ladies," he whispered. "Let me serve you instead. We shall have an interesting time while I try to take off these many skirts of yours. I'm sure they were fashioned to deter all but the strongest of men from sleeping with their wives!"

She stood obediently still until at last she was left with only her long hair to cover her nakedness. Edmund's hands were warm and gentle as they caressed her slowly and deliberately.

"White and beautiful. Such skin I've never seen before. It is like silk." He drew her towards the bed. "Come, I will give you the son we both desire, and the making of the child will be a great joy."

His lips were eager and she responded to the warmth in him. Love flowed through her as it always did when he caressed her and she clung to him, her head pressed against his swiftly beating heart.

He held her in an almost suffocating embrace and Margaret felt a fierce pain that brought joy in its wake, and she cried tears of happiness because she was Edmund's wife and he found her desirable.

The crisp spring air slanted in through the windows and already the trees were covered in buds with the warm promise of summer mellowing the sun.

Edmund leaned his bright head against the tapestries that hung on the wall, playing sweet music to Margaret and singing to her in his native Welsh that she found so beautiful.

As the sounds of music fell away, Margaret took her husband's hand.

"That was lovely, my lord, but so sad. See, you have brought tears to my eyes."

He moved away from her and went to the window and a sudden fear caught at her heart. She followed him and leaned against his broad back, her head against the softness of his doublet.

"Edmund, you frighten me with your silence. Please tell me what is wrong."

He turned and took her in his arms. "Silly wife, nothing is wrong; but though it may be fine to sit here like a little lapdog and be waited on hand and foot, I must think some time of my duties to the King."

She drew herself from his arms and stood upright, her head high. "Edmund, don't humour me, I wish to know what is really going through your mind."

He smiled warmly. "You are quite right, my perceptive little wife. You have a right to know what is happening." He took both her hands in his. "Richard of York, together with Salisbury and Warwick, is planning to march on London. Somerset is to be sent out to apprehend the rebel faction."

Margaret shook her head. "Why does Richard act so? He was such a gentleman the night he visited us."

"He feels his cause is just!" Edmund said simply. "He may be mistaken, but he is quite sincere, and to his mind the Yorkists are the most fit to rule England." He kissed the up-turned palms of her hand. "Come, my lady, enough of such talk. We have more important things to concern ourselves with. Isn't it time we went to our beds?"

Margaret's cheeks were rosy as she glanced up at him from under her lashes and then out of the window.

"But, my lord, it is afternoon, and the sun still shines. See how high it is over the gardens!"

Giggling, she turned and ran from him, closing the door of the bedchamber with a resounding bang. For a moment she thought he had taken her words seriously, then there was a gentle knock on the door.

"Edmund of Richmond wishes to enter his bedchamber only to find his wife has locked it against him," he said loudly.

Margaret gave a little scream of embarrassment and opened the door quickly.

"How could you, Edmund," she said softly, "what will everyone think?"

She caught his sleeve and pulled him inside the chamber. He laughed and caught her up in his arms, kissing her lips warmly.

"Oh, dearest husband." Margaret nibbled his ear gently running her hands through the thick vibrant hair that hung down to his collar. "Will we always be in love like this, do you think?" She wriggled free so that she could stare into his eyes.

Fiercely he pressed her close to him, his eyes closed as if in pain. He carried her to the bed and took her quickly, as if afraid there would be no tomorrows for them to enjoy each other.

Margaret sensed his mood and she clung to him tightly, her thin arms holding him so close as if never to let him go. Finally, they lay exhausted, side by side, hands entwined in an unbreakable bond.

"Margaret," Edmund said with quiet fervour, "I will love you with all my heart and so long as there is breath left in my body. When I no longer love you, I will be dead."

CHAPTER EIGHT

"When will it be over?" Margaret paced the room impatiently, her hands twisting knots into her white kerchief. "Surely there must be news soon. I just can't bear this waiting."

For the hundredth time she turned to the window, searching the sunlit fields for any sign that the Earl of Richmond may be returning.

"Please, Margaret, won't you try to rest?" Elizabeth pleaded. "There will be news before much longer, I'm sure."

In reality she was sure of nothing, save the heavy dark shadows under Margaret's young eyes, and the thinness of her small-boned face.

She had watched the tension grow in Margaret ever since the Earl had ridden out for St. Albans to join the King in battle. She could eat nothing, not even the cold meats spread with jelly that she loved so much. The most she would take was a little thin soup sprinkled with parsley and now she stood like a small slim child, lost without her husband's love and comfort.

Suddenly she gave a cry. "Look, Elizabeth, horsemen on the long meadow!" She stood on a stool and leaned over the sill, careless of the danger. "I cannot tell from here if Edmund is among them!" she said distractedly. "They all look alike in their gleaming helmets. I will go down to the doors and await them there."

Elizabeth hastened to her side. "Careful of the steps, Margaret, it would not do for you to suffer a fall." But Margaret was away, her skirts flying behind her as she sped downwards.

She was outside then, with the sun all around her and a rider was detaching himself from the army of men.

He leaned down and scooped Margaret into his arms and there was such a look of holy joy in her face that Elizabeth felt the tears choke in her own throat. She stepped back into the coolness of the doorway. Margaret would not heed her for some time, nothing was more certain. She would not leave her husband's side. She brushed impatiently at the foolish tears and slowly returned to her own chamber.

The fire threw great shadows along the walls and the room was all the more comfortable because of the light spring rain that pattered like thousands of tiny feet on the courtyard outside.

Edmund sat stretched to his full length, his feet towards the burning logs, the weariness gradually disappearing from his face.

Margaret slipped down on to the small stool at his side and rested her head against his knee.

"Was the battle very terrible, Edmund?" She took his hand and held it tightly against her breast.

"Bad enough, Margaret," he sighed. "Your uncle, the Duke of Somerset, lost his life, as did Northumberland and Lord Clifford." He stretched out his hand and caressed Margaret's cheek. "These are hard times. You will need courage, my little one."

Margaret held her hand to her lips and closed her eyes. There was a deep sorrow inside her that her father's brother was now dead on the field of battle. She thought of her three young cousins — strong, sturdy young men, but how they would miss the love and guidance of their father.

"What of the King?" she said at last, her heart beating faster with the fear growing within her.

"He was taken prisoner, but York will not do him any harm. He will not seek to usurp the position of the Prince of Wales."

"What will happen then?" Margaret looked at Edmund fearfully. "Will Richard of York try to capture you?"

Edmund smiled. "I don't think he'll bother about the Tudors! He does not consider us enough of a threat to him. At least not yet." He paused for a moment, his eyes regarding Margaret steadily. "He may, of course, decide that we are dangerous if we have a son, you and I."

Margaret shook her head. "How could that make a difference? The King has a son and heir of his own."

"Our child would be of royal blood, don't forget. Both from the Beaufort line and from my mother, Queen Catherine de Valois. In certain circumstances, such a boy could be a threat."

Margaret shuddered. "It makes me fearful of

bearing a child." She was silent for a moment, watching the flickering firelight illumine Edmund's strong face and bright hair. "What will happen now?" she asked at last, wishing that the affairs of the country had no power to touch her life with Edmund.

"Richard of York will probably assume the position of the King's chief aide, in place of Somerset. He will, no doubt, be received on to the council and that will bring him one step nearer the throne."

Margaret pressed herself closer to her husband, aware of the warmth of his body against her own.

"And what of us?" she said softly. "What shall we do?"

She wound her arms around him, and he took her face in both his hands and kissed her on the mouth. She felt tremors of joy speed through her, and she closed her eyes, drinking in the nearness of him.

"Suddenly my weariness has vanished," he said, smiling. "I shall show you how much I love you and how much I've missed you."

He lifted her easily in his arms and carried her into the chamber. She lay back against the pillows, feeling the fluttering mixture of joy and fear that his physical needs always aroused in her.

He held her fiercely, but his mouth was gentle as it explored her neck and the pinkness of her small nipples. She sighed and wound her arms around him, delighting in the hard muscles of his back arched above her. And then they were one, and tears of happiness spilled on to her cheeks.

Edmund was truly hers once more.

Pembroke Castle rose high and indomitable against the pale evening sky, its sheer majesty, as it clung to the cliffs overlooking the sea, took Margaret's breath away.

"Do you like its splendour?" Edmund bent to look down at her and Margaret smiled her delight in spite of the ache in her bones from the long journey. "Here I will plant my son within you, and he will be born on Welsh soil. You will both prosper at Pembroke, I feel it strongly."

As they entered under the archway of mellow stones, Margaret knew she had come to a place she could love as she'd loved Bletsoe when she was a child.

Edmund was drawing her into the warmth of the great hall and she was suddenly surrounded by tall handsome men.

"Father!" Edmund went forward and embraced Owen Tudor who still had the handsomeness that had once caught the heart of the Queen of England.

He came to her and smiled, his eyes bright and clear, his grip strong as he kissed her cheek.

"Welcome to Pembroke, my daughter," he said, in a deep voice that was vibrant with emotion. "You must always look on this place as your home, because there will always be a welcome for you in the House of Tudor."

Jasper came forward and pressed her hand warmly, his dark eyes alight. "Margaret, how good to see you. Come; be seated. You no doubt feel tired after your journey." He shook back his hair that was as bright as Edmund's. "Our land is beautiful, but sometimes wild and uncomfortable for travellers. We would not have it otherwise. The safety of Pembroke Castle is in its position above the sea."

Margaret felt her tiredness slip away from her. She was enchanted by the tall handsome Tudors, masters in their own little world far away from the intrigues of the English Court. Here in the wild hills of Wales, they were a law unto themselves, as tough and hard as the stonework of the castle itself.

That night, she lay with Edmund listening to the waves lapping the far wall. It was a gentle sound, but then the spring breeze was soft and light and carried little weight. What of the winter when the winds shrieked to a fury outside the walls? She imagined the dark green sea dashing itself endlessly against the rocky fortress, and shivered in spite of the warmth of Edmund's arm around her.

Margaret's fingers became slow over her tapestry, the needle poised as she listened to Owen Tudor talking to his sons. She watched as he nodded his proud head, giving emphasis to what he had been saying.

She often spent her time in such a fashion. It interested her greatly to hear Owen speak of his days in the army of Henry the Fifth of England.

Elizabeth had kept to her bed since the journey into Wales. She had caught a severe chill, and Margaret insisted that she take the utmost care of herself so that her recovery would be all the quicker. She smiled to herself, recalling that even in her feverish condition, Elizabeth had taken a moment to admire the tall Welshmen of Pembroke. No doubt she would take every opportunity to enjoy their company once she had recovered from her indisposition.

Margaret stretched her fingers. They had grown cold and cramped through holding her needle. She put down her tapestry and rose to her feet, and immediately the eyes of her husband were upon her. She swayed a little, and Edmund was at her side, holding her carefully.

"What is it, Margaret, are you ill?" he said, anxiously. "It could be that you have caught a fever from Elizabeth. You should not try to play the nurse always."

Her head cleared and she looked up into his bright blue eyes, a smile curving her lips.

"I am not ill," she said softly. "I am with child."

She knew the colour was high in her cheeks as Edmund drew her nearer to the fire. His eyes were almost dark in the sudden joy that was reflected in the faces of his father and brother as they all stood and looked down at her, so that she felt like a delicate engraved figure.

"It is quite a usual happening," she said, smiling. "I have done nothing out of the ordinary. It is just that I'm going to be a mother."

Owen kissed her fingers with grave courtesy. "My dear daughter, I am so happy for you and for myself too. I need a grandson."

She realised with a catch of her breath that there were tears in his eyes, and that Owen was moved more than he could say by her news.

Edmund tenderly led her to a chair and arranged a cushion at her back and one beneath her feet.

"I am a strong young woman," she said, smiling. "I assure you I will not break at a touch."

Owen rested a hand lightly on her shoulder. His face held a faraway look, and for a moment Margaret was afraid.

"This boy that you carry within you will make England a safe and prosperous place," he said soberly. "You must guard him well. He has a great destiny to fulfil."

Margaret shuddered a little, thinking unwillingly of the old woman who had sheltered her from the mob at London Bridge. She had foretold that Margaret's son would rule England. Could Owen Tudor think so too?

But no, it was impossible! King Henry the Sixth still lived, and his son was lusty and strong. Even in the event of a double tragedy in the royal family, Richard of York and his heirs would be next in line for the throne.

She shook away the feeling of gloom that had descended for a moment, and smiled up at her husband, clasping his hand in hers.

"I want no more from life than I have at this moment," she said earnestly. "My husband at my side and my child growing within me."

Edmund forbade her now to ride even the most docile mare along the rugged coastline, and instead she contented herself with a gentle walk on the golden sands that curved like a smiling mouth against the darkness of the rocks.

She had come to love Pembroke Castle, and she knew that the Welsh people were making up charming rhymes about the love match between herself and Edmund. She was proud that the fierce, brave inhabitants of the surrounding villages had taken her to their hearts.

The days were soft and sunlit, each one imprinted itself on her mind and was stored away in her memory.

The peace was not to last! It was shattered quite suddenly when Owen who had been keeping watch on the battlements, saw a dark snake-line of soldiers wending their way over the hills.

"Come, boys, we have visitors!" There was excitement in his voice and his hair stood around his head like a silver halo.

Margaret hurried after them up the steep stone steps and Edmund turned back to reprove her.

"Take your time, Margaret," he said gently. "Think of our son."

Nevertheless, he took her arm and helped her the rest of the way.

"Look!" Owen's voice rang out. "It is the royal standard, the King himself is coming to Pembroke!"

But it was the Queen who entered through the great archway. Margaret heard her strident voice, thickly accented as she called commands to her escort, and her spirits sank.

She knew instinctively that Queen Margaret of Anjou had not come to spend a quiet time listening to the musicians playing the sweet Welsh airs that so charmed her own leisure hours. More than likely she had come with some new strategy of war that she wished to discuss at length with Jasper and Edmund.

Margaret sighed softly. The peaceful summer was over.

"You seem despondent, my love. Perhaps you are tired?"

Margaret drew Edmund away from the press of people in the great hall and he went with her thankfully to the peace of their own chamber.

"Where Her Majesty finds her strength and vigour is beyond me." He smiled, reassuringly patting Margaret's hand. "Don't frown so, this fatigue is the result of too many rich banquets and much too much dancing late into the night."

Margaret sat beside him taking his hand and

holding it to her cheek.

"I wish you would care more about your health, Edmund," she reproached gently. "That cough of yours becomes worse, I'm sure of it."

"Nonsense!" he smiled warmly. "Look at my father. Have you ever seen a man his age look so fit? We are a strong family, my love."

"Nevertheless, I insist that you stay in bed tomorrow and rest. I don't like the shadows that have come under your eyes."

He leaned forward and kissed her. "Your belly grows round and your heart grows softer as a mother's should, but don't be too tender, little Margaret. Come to bed. I'm sure no one will miss us from the revelries for once."

Long after, Edmund's regular breathing told Margaret that he was asleep. She lay watching the flickering shadows dance along the walls. Her heart was heavy with fear, even though she didn't know what was causing her distress.

She was just on the edge of sleep when she heard the heavy accented voice of the Queen outside the door.

"Jasper, hold me close. You do not know how much it means to me to have your strong arms around me once more." There was silence for a moment, and then the Queen spoke again. "I cannot exist without you, my love. You must come back to Court soon, promise me."

Jasper spoke then. "I will be with you at Court as soon as I can. The Tudors will be a thorn in the flesh of Richard of York that he will not remove easily."

"You talk of war and I know well enough what a brave soldier you are, but what of me? Don't you think of me as a woman sometimes?"

"I think of nothing else!" Jasper's voice faded and Margaret knew that he had moved away towards the Queen's chambers.

She lay still, wondering what Owen Tudor would do if he knew that his first born son was making love to the Queen of England. Still, it was none of her business. She turned towards the warmth of her husband and tried to sleep.

He stirred and turning, took her in his arms and as she clung to him, all thoughts of Jasper and the Queen were thrust from her mind as she realised how laboured his breathing had become. Under her hands, his shoulders felt thin and she sat up, staring into his face, as it dawned on her that her beloved Edmund was ill.

CHAPTER NINE

Autumn mists swept inwards from the sea, encircling Pembroke Castle in white, vaporous arms, and Margaret watched Edmund slowly but surely lose his strength. She spent hours in supplication to the Holy Mother, disregarding the discomfort of her body full with child.

Edmund remained in his bed most days, his hands pale and thin as they rested against the covers. But his hair was a bright flag of defiance around his hollow face.

"So lay his mother," Owen said, his eyes dark with anguish, "just before she died."

"No!" Margaret said fiercely. "Edmund will not die. I could not live my life without him."

Owen embraced her then, staring down compassionately at her from his great height.

"We must all bend to the will of the saints, my child. We cannot change the course of our destiny. But be of good courage. Edmund is young and strong. He may be spared."

Margaret drew away from him, frightened by the doubt in Owen's voice. She pulled a woollen shawl around her shoulders and ventured on to the coarse common land outside the castle walls. Perhaps if she gathered some herbs and made an infusion for him to drink, he might regain his strength.

Her back ached as she bent over, seeking

among the strong grass for the necessary ingredients for the potion that would heal Edmund, but she searched on, unaware of the rough seas and the screeching gulls that wheeled overhead.

When she brought him the cup, he drank obediently, reaching out thin fingers towards her.

"Hold my hand, Margaret. Keep me company for a while. Soon I will grow vigorous and eager to give you more sons."

She sat beside him at once and cradled his head against her full body.

"There," she said softly. "Do you feel our son moving within me? You will be well long before he is born."

She closed her eyes to hide the tears that sprung so readily to the surface. She was ashamed of her weakness and sent up a silent prayer for strength.

Time had no meaning for Margaret, and she failed to notice that the mists had turned to bitter cold rain and howling winds that sent tapers flickering in grotesque shapes along the stone walls.

Elizabeth grew concerned and urged her to rest. "Think of your son, Margaret. You will do him harm if you don't take care of yourself."

But nothing would induce Margaret to leave Edmund's side. She said her morning prayers at an altar set up near at hand, lighting candles with meticulous care. She would hand one to Edmund so that even in their devotions they were together.

But the day came when he could not even hold the candle she brought him. His hollow cheeks had taken on a bluish translucence, and slowly Margaret went to Elizabeth.

"Bring his father and Jasper. Tell them to come with all haste, or they will be too late."

She returned to the bedside and sat with her husband, holding his cold frail hands in her own.

His lips moved a little. "Care for our son. He will be above other men." He closed his eyes then, and it was over.

Dry-eyed, Margaret pulled the covers up around him as if to warm him even in death, and turned calmly to Owen.

"My husband is dead," she said flatly, and Jasper hurried to the bedside, his face drawn with grief. Head high, Margaret turned from the room. "I will be alone for a time," she said wearily and without once turning back, she left the chamber of death.

They buried him in the church of Grey Friars, in the sweet fresh soil of Carmarthen. November rain washed down the mountainside as if the heavens were shedding tears that Margaret could not.

"I have bade one of my officers write an elegy." Jasper drew her arm through his, supporting her against his strength. "Glyn Gothi writes from the heart. He loved Edmund well."

Margaret stared at the headstone, unable to read the Welsh words that danced before her eyes, and somehow it didn't matter. Edmund was dead and no amount of fine words would bring him back to her.

She turned heavily away from the churchyard, her eyes blinded by rain. "Goodbye, my love," she whispered, and holding her shoulders erect, walked between the rain-clean graves.

Pembroke was a silent place in the days that followed the burial service. Jasper had gone away to London, unable to bear the dark shadowy memories of his brother, and Owen sat before the huge fire in silent grief that could find no words.

Only Elizabeth was able to maintain some semblance of normality. She chattered unceasingly about the rumours that filtered through to Wales from the Court, and brought Margaret tempting morsels of food, urging her to eat if only for the sake of the child.

Then in the space of a few weeks, the unborn infant seemed to gain strength. He moved with vigour that took Margaret's breath away.

"Look Elizabeth!" she said in astonishment. "My child is strong, is he not?"

She sat before the window, seeing how beautiful the fields had become under a mantle of snow, and with both her hands placed on her swollen stomach, she was comforted.

"The King is seized with madness once again!" Jasper flung off his cloak, his bright hair clinging wetly to his strong face. "Now York will have all the power he could wish for, except that

117

he does not hold the crown itself."

Margaret's heart was beating hard. For a moment, when Jasper had come in so unexpectedly, she could almost imagine it was Edmund standing there, weary and mud-stained from the journey.

She went forward slowly just as Owen, with a shout of greeting, came down into the great hall.

"How was the Court, my son? Full of intrigues as usual, I have no doubt."

The two men clasped hands, and Jasper flung back his head and laughed.

"What's a man to do when his father asks a question and then makes his own answer?" he said, smiling at Margaret.

All at once her spirits lightened. Jasper with his fresh youthfulness had brought life once more into the grey walls of Pembroke. He kissed her cheeks and appraised her roundness.

"Soon the child will be born. I am happy to be here for the great event. No doubt you've been holding back, waiting for my arrival?"

She laughed and clung to him for a moment, closing her eyes, pretending for a fraction of a moment that it was Edmund holding her.

"I am beginning to think I will never have the child," she said lightly. "It seems he is waiting for warmer weather."

Jasper sat before the fire and stretched out his long legs, sighing with contentment.

"It is very good to be home," he said. "And London is for the moment at peace, even though it be an uneasy one. Soon there is to be a procession to Saint Paul's to pray for the souls of those slain in battle at St. Albans."

Margaret looked down at her slippers, watching the mingling of colours reflected from the firelight, wondering how many widows were grieving, even as she grieved, for husbands that were gone from them.

"But the Queen will never allow matters to rest there," Jasper said with certainty. "Queen Margaret of Anjou is not called the 'she-wolf' for nothing, as York will find out."

Margaret looked at Jasper fearfully. "But if the Queen causes friction, surely the war will start up again?"

He nodded. "It will. And we Tudors will be up to our necks in it."

Margaret's fluttering hands rested for a moment on her stomach. What would become of her child if Owen and Jasper were to be slain in battle?

Owen seemed to read into her very mind. "Don't you worry about us, Margaret. We are tough. And I, the old bird, is the toughest of the lot! We will come to no harm." He placed his large hand over hers. "The King is not beaten yet. He will regain his senses once more as he's done in the past, and then York will find his place."

All at once Margaret was unendurably tired. She pushed herself out of the chair with difficulty and stood swaying a little.

"I must go to my bed. Forgive me for not being better company on your first night home, Jasper. Perhaps the morning will find me more rested. I'd like it very much if we could talk then."

She kissed them both and left them sitting near the fire, talking endlessly about the wars.

Margaret woke to the still darkness of the night and it was as if a band of steel encircled her body.

"Elizabeth!" she called urgently. "I think my time has come."

Elizabeth, her face white, hurriedly rose from her bed, pulling a robe around her shoulders.

"God and all the saints, Margaret, you could have chosen a warmer night."

Margaret tried to smile, but the pain was too great. It was as if the bones of her spine were being drawn apart inch by inch.

When she opened her eyes once more, the pain had receded and she could breathe again. She realised then she had been holding tightly to Elizabeth's hands — so tightly that her nails had drawn blood.

Gently Elizabeth drew away. "I will call the midwife. She will have things under control."

Soon it seemed the chamber was full. Dim figures brought brighter tapers and the midwife, round and rosy-checked, talked soothingly in Welsh, doing strange things with clean capable hands.

The pain was rising again, mercilessly gripping Margaret's body in red-hot fingers. She tried to lift her mind above it, praying to the saints for help through her ordeal. But the soft moans continued to escape from her tightly pressed lips.

Elizabeth came and stood before her, waiting for the spasm to recede.

"Look, Margaret. See how fine and small the clothes are. Soon your baby will be born and we will dress him so warmly that the cold wind will not possibly touch him."

Margaret nodded; her strength was ebbing away, but she saw how the gentlewoman's hand shook as she held the tiny garments up for inspection.

Owen was bending over her, then, his fine handsome face furrowed with concern.

"Be brave little Margaret," he said gently. "Soon there will be another Tudor in Pembroke Castle."

Margaret tried to speak, but floods of darkness threatened to overwhelm her. Faces swam away from her and in that instant she could see, as if in a mist, the old woman of London Bridge.

"Courage, my lady," she seemed to be saying. "The King of England is about to be born."

Fresh courage came to Margaret then and she braced herself to complete the struggle so that her son would come into the world all the more quickly. She knew beforehand that she would have a son and that he would be the image of his father.

CHAPTER TEN

The grey light of dawn was creeping slowly into the chamber when Margaret opened her eyes. She felt curiously fresh and well-rested and when she placed her hands on her body, her stomach was flat underneath the binding of linen.

A great fire crackled in the hearth, sending out hissing sounds with an occasional crack of shifting logs. Margaret sighed contentedly and turned to look at the crib that rocked gently under the hand of a nurse.

"Good morning, Margaret; the air is still a little chill, but I think we will have some winter sunshine later in the day."

Elizabeth stood at her side, a steaming bowl in her hand. She seated herself on the edge of the bed and held a spoon to Margaret's lips.

"Come, take some gruel. It will make you strong again. You'll need your strength to look after that hefty son of yours."

Margaret struggled to sit up. "It is the feast of St. Agnes, is it not?" she smiled. "The twenty-eighth day of January, the day my son was born."

As if to emphasise her words, the child began to cry, great gasping sobs that tore at Margaret's heart.

"Bring him to me," she said softly, and after a moment's hesitation, Elizabeth lifted the child and brought him over to the bed.

He stopped crying as soon as he was placed in Margaret's arms and she held his tiny fingers to her lips in an ecstasy of joy.

"His hair is bright like his father's," she whispered, and tears stole down her cheeks. "See how his little fingers curl against mine."

Elizabeth bent towards her. "Do not tire yourself, Margaret. Let me return him to his crib."

Margaret stared down at her son for a long moment, reluctant to let him go from her arms. "I shall call him Henry," she smiled through her tears. "Edmund would have approved of his son being named for the King."

She allowed Elizabeth to take the baby from her and sank back wearily against the pillows.

"I have the strangest feeling, Elizabeth." She closed her eyes against the pale morning light, brushing the strands of hair from her forehead. "I shall never bear another child! My son will have no one but me to love him in his infancy."

"Nonsense!" Elizabeth said briskly. "You are little more than a child yourself. Thirteen summers is not very ancient, I do assure you." She straightened the covers and plumped up the bolster behind Margaret's head. "In time you will learn to grow fond of someone else and no doubt you will marry and have a large family. You once said it was what you desired."

Margaret shook her head. "That was when Edmund was alive. I know now that there will be no other children, and no man I will ever love as

I loved my husband." She smiled at Elizabeth's disconcerted expression. "There is no need to fret about it. I am content with my son. I will live for him and do my utmost to make up to him for his lack of a father." She sighed gently. "I think I will try to sleep, and when I am more rested, I will nurse my child."

She drifted off to sleep and though there were tears drying on her cheeks, she was smiling.

Lionel, Lord Welles, looked up in admiration at the towering walls of Pembroke Castle, noticing that the sea protecting the outer wall was azure in the sun.

He smiled at his wife. "Soon, my dear, you will see your grandson for the first time, though to me the idea is absurd. You are far too young and beautiful to be a grandmother."

The Duchess of Somerset sighed deeply. "I feel quite old after the difficulties we've endured on the journey. I am only thankful that we left our own young son at home."

The retinue passed under the archway of stone and there waiting on the steps of the castle was Margaret surrounded by the towering Tudor men. The Duchess saw with pride that her daughter was now an elegant young woman, a little thin and pale perhaps, but that was natural enough in the circumstances.

"Mother!" Margaret hurried across the yard, her gown fluttering in the breeze. "Welcome to Pembroke." She kissed her mother's cheek and turned to Lord Welles, a happy smile on her face. "Lionel, you are just as handsome as I remembered you, and not looking a day older."

She took his arm, feeling a flood of affection for the big gentleman who had taken her father's place. They went immediately to the nurseries where the baby lay asleep, his bright hair jutting from beneath his bonnet and his cheeks healthy and firm.

"Oh, he is so handsome." The Duchess bent over him, seeing immediately the likeness the boy bore to his dead father. Her eyes met Margaret's and her daughter smiled.

"I know what you are thinking, mother," she said softly. "He is very much like Edmund, and I am glad of it."

The Duchess took Margaret's arm and led her away from the crowd of people gathered around the crib.

"Listen to me, Margaret," she said, and though she spoke quietly, there was a note of urgency in her voice. "I was bereft when your father, the Duke, died suddenly and in such tragic circumstances. But life must go on." She stared at Margaret steadily. "A woman needs a man's protection and so when I met Leo, I married him."

Margaret's eyes were withdrawn, and her mother rushed on nervously.

"Think about your son. His future would be more secure with a father to protect his interests."

Quietly Margaret settled herself into a chair as if her legs would no longer support her.

"My son has his grandfather, Owen Tudor, to care for him. And Jasper who would lay down his life for the boy. What more could he want?"

The Duchess sighed. "I will say just one more thing on the subject, and thereafter hold my tongue. The Tudors are a breed of fighters and a country in such a state of unrest as ours gobbles up such men. Believe me, when I say that you need a husband of your own!"

There was a silence that lengthened into minutes while Margaret considered her answer. At last she rose to her feet with such a gesture of weariness that the Duchess felt a deep pity for her.

"Come, let us talk of other matters," she said quickly. "You are so young and have many years ahead of you. I am forgetting how near your grief must still be." She patted Margaret's arm awkwardly. "Let me hold the little one for just a moment. I promise not to spoil him too much while I'm here."

She was rewarded by a smile then, and with a sense of relief the Duchess turned once more towards the baby lying asleep in his crib.

The Duchess of Somerset lost no time in approaching Owen Tudor about the future of her daughter.

"I am naturally concerned that she and the boy should have every advantage, my lord," she smiled at him in her charming way, and Margaret could see that Owen admired her mother greatly.

He turned to Margaret. "It is only right that you consider your future," he said gently. "Naturally the boy will inherit his father's estate and the title of Earl of Richmond, but you are young enough to make an advantageous marriage." He coughed a little in embarrassment. "You will always have a home at Pembroke Castle. You must understand that we love you here, as if you were our own flesh and blood." He looked at Jasper who nodded in fervent agreement. "But I could find you a good Lancastrian who would care for you and young Henry, and guard you with his life."

The Duchess smiled graciously, pleased to have brought the matter into the open. It was obvious that the menfolk would have been content to allow circumstances to remain as they were indefinitely.

That night, Margaret huddled dry-eyed in her bed, staring at the flickering shapes thrown by the tapers on to the walls. She had only just begun to grow accustomed to the emptiness of her life without Edmund, and now her mother, with the best of intentions, had succeeded in opening old wounds.

She thought of the cold wet day barely six months ago when Edmund had been laid to rest in the dark earth and closed her eyes tightly against the pain of it. She could not bear to take another husband. Her mother didn't begin to know what she was asking.

She slipped from the covers on to the coldness of the floor, and bowed her head in prayer.

"Help me to do what is right and to be an obedient daughter and a gracious mother," she whispered, but her heart still ached and her arms still longed to embrace her beloved Edmund.

The castle seemed silent and empty. Darkness fell early, and morning seemed late arriving.

Margaret sat at the high window, her tapestry fallen unnoticed to the floor. She tried to occupy her mind with the beauty of the rolling fields sloping down towards the roughness of the sea. Rocks surfaced from the foaming breakers like slippery black dogs, and then were hidden again as the deep swelling tide raced with frightening speed against the shore.

Across the mountain path new grass had sprung, so that the road had almost vanished, and every day Margaret sat watching, waiting for a sign that Owen and Jasper were returning home.

The wars had started up once more with frightening suddenness; the Queen had taken matters into her own impulsive hands. She had sent out Lord Audley to arrest Salisbury who was attempting to join Richard of York at Ludlow. Affairs had not turned out to her expectation, and Audley had been killed.

As soon as Owen and Jasper heard the news,

they had set out for England with as many men as they could muster, and now were probably marching on Ludlow with the King, who had once more recovered his senses.

"Margaret, I'm sorry to interrupt you, but the young Earl continues to cry. His nurse thinks he may be feverish."

Elizabeth stood at Margaret's side, her broad face lined with concern.

"I will come at once." Margaret tried to speak calmly, but fear pounded within her so that she could hardly breathe.

She hurried into the nursery that was kept warm day and night to keep out the damp air that the sea sometimes brought inland.

The baby was turning restlessly to and fro in his bed, and Margaret took him up, gently cradling him in her arms. He was indeed feverish and beads of perspiration stood like tiny jewels on his cheeks and forehead.

"There, there," she crooned softly, "mother will make you better, don't cry. Bring some cool water, Elizabeth," she said quietly, "and open the drapes so that some freshness can enter the room."

Margaret continued to hold him long after it was necessary, staring down at the small features that were so like Edmund's.

"Was my mother right?" she wondered out loud. "Do I owe it to you to marry again and give you a new father?"

She thought of the happiness she herself had

found with Lord Welles to be a father to tease her and comfort her when she cried. Suddenly there were tears, but now there was no bitterness, only a calming acceptance that Edmund was gone from her for ever, and she must make a new life for herself and her son.

"They are coming, Margaret!" Elizabeth called urgently from her seat in the high window. "I can see their helmets gleaming in the sun. The men are home from the wars!"

Margaret swept young Henry up in her arms and he waved plump fists in excitement, as she hurried to look across the mountainside.

"Thank God!" she said fervently. "I can see the Tudor standard flying high. They must both be safe." She swung away from the window with a burst of happiness. "Go and tell the cooks to prepare a fine feast. My Lord Tudor will be here within the hour."

Henry clapped his hands and pushed away from his mother's arms to toddle precariously across the room. He laughed aloud with glee, infected by the air of excitement, even though he did not understand its cause.

"Go with your nurse, and let her dress you in your best doublet!" Margaret scolded with a smile on her lips, and Henry allowed himself to be lifted up and taken to the nursery.

Margaret looked down at her own dress. It was time she discarded her dark gowns and wore something bright and becoming. Excitedly, she opened her closet and chose a deep blue gown of fine velvet edged with frills of white lace.

"Bring my comb, Elizabeth," she said gaily. "We will give them a homecoming they will never forget."

The tables in the great hall were laden with food and still servants scurried to and fro, bringing yet more delicacies to tempt the daintiest appetite.

Great swans, browned to succulent tenderness and garnished with pounded ginger and dried violet leaves, had pride of place on the main table, while along the sides of the room stood the steaming dishes of fish cooked in ale and spread with almonds. Bowls of eggs beaten with chopped dittany and coloured to a deep yellow with the addition of saffron, stood like eyes among the beets and crisp lettuce.

"A feast fit for a king!" Owen strode into the hall, tall and handsome as ever, and at his side, Jasper smiled in delight at the scene of welcome. "You have done well, Margaret." He bent over her hand and she returned his smile warmly.

Owen turned and drew forward a young man, slight of frame and sallow of complexion who, nonetheless, had an air of distinction about his bearing.

"This is Henry Stafford," Owen said, "Second son of the Duke of Buckingham, and a fine Lancastrian if ever there was one."

Margaret felt her colour rise as she understood the implication of his words.

"Come, be seated," she said quickly. "You must all be tired and hungry after the long journey."

Somehow young Stafford contrived to sit beside her and he insisted on helping her to something from every dish until she began to laugh in spite of herself.

"If I listened to you, my lord, I would soon be too big to sit behind the table," she protested.

At last the great banquet was over and Margaret led the way into the smaller chamber with its cheerful fire of logs.

"Now, my lords, are you going to tell me about the battle?" she said impishly, knowing it would be more than she could do to try and stop them.

"The Yorkists have fled in all directions," Owen said with satisfaction. "The King's prompt action in marching to Lydlow confounded them all. York himself has fled to Ireland. It appears that he was once deputy there, so relies on the Irishmen to hide him." He leaned back in his chair, stretching his long legs wearily before him. "Salisbury and Warwick have made for Calais, taking the young Earl of March with them."

Margaret was immediately concerned. "Oh, how could Richard of York bear to be parted from his son? Could he not have gone to Calais with him?"

Owen gave a short laugh. "On the field of battle, it is every man for himself, and the Earl of March may be young, but he's a man for all that!

I'll say that much for him." He stretched his big arms above his head. "If you'll forgive an old man, Margaret, I must go to my bed. I'm so tired I can hardly move."

"So full of good food you mean!" Jasper said with a laugh. "But perhaps you are right. It is time I retired too. I'll see you in the morning, Margaret, and mayhap you will let me take my young nephew riding, if the weather is fine."

Margaret felt a dart of fear. Henry was still just a baby. The idea of him being placed upon the back of a great horse was disturbing, to say the least.

"I'll guard him well, have no fear," Jasper said gently, and Margaret thought of the welcome her son had received from Jasper earlier, when, dusty and tired, he had ridden into the castle yard.

There had been an instant feeling between the tough soldier and her small son; she had felt it strongly as Jasper had lifted Henry in his arms, holding him tenderly against his strong shoulder.

"Of course he can go with you," she said, quickly ashamed of her hesitation. She did not want her son to grow up into a mother's boy, did she?

It was quiet after the Tudor men had left the chamber and Margaret was sunk into her own thoughts, almost dozing a little before the warmth of the fire when she realised that Lord Stafford was at her side.

"You must forgive my rudeness," she said quickly, "I did not think. I should be treating you like a guest, and here I am almost asleep."

"You are forgiven," Henry Stafford said, bowing over her hand, his green eyes alight with admiration. He stared at her for a long moment until she raised her eyebrows quizically. "Now it is my turn to beg your pardon." He laughed, and it was a pleasant sound. "You are so much younger than I thought; why, you are little more than a girl. About fifteen years, if I'm any judge."

"I feel much older, I do assure you," Margaret said truthfully, indicating that he take a seat beside her. "What brings you to Pembroke, my lord?"

He coloured a little under her direct gaze and she softened towards him, smiling so warmly that he took his courage in both hands.

"I did not intend to speak so soon, but I would much rather be open about my intentions," he said. "I am here to ask you to become my wife." He held up his hand to stop her speaking. "I am no great catch," he admitted. "But even though I am a second son, my father has settled a great deal of his estate upon me, and I vow I would always be kind to you and to the young Earl of Richmond."

Margaret was touched in spite of the fear that made her heart beat fast. How could she bear to take another man for husband after loving Edmund so much? She tried to imagine herself in Stafford's arms; in his bed.

She rose abruptly. "I must have time," she said quickly. "Marriage is not a matter to enter into lightly, I am sure you will agree with me."

He stood beside her, not touching her, but his eyes were clear as they looked into hers.

"I know already that I could love you well, my lady, and if you will allow me, I will defend you with my life."

Margaret looked down at her hands. "Please, let me think," she said softly, and then he had gathered her hands in his and she was surprised at his strength.

"Think all you like, Margaret, but I am determined to make you my wife."

He left her then and she stood before the logs that gleamed richly, reminding her of the colour of Edmund's hair, and tears blurred her eyes.

"What am I to do?" she whispered piteously, but the silent walls gave back no answer.

CHAPTER ELEVEN

"The King has called a Parliament at Coventry."

Henry Stafford slipped off his cloak and a shower of dust fell, only to be imprisoned in the shaft of sunlight from the open door.

"You have ridden hard, my lord. Let me bring you some wine while you settle yourself before the fire."

Margaret drew him into the body of the hall, seeing with concern the lines of fatigue that had become etched on his thin face.

He smiled at her. "I enjoy your solicitude, my lady, and I will be grateful for refreshments. It will lay the dust in my throat."

When she had filled his cup for the second time, Margaret settled herself beside him.

"Come, tell me all the news. I can hardly bear the suspense a moment longer."

Henry Stafford looked down into his cup. "Richard of York has been attainted." He took a quick drink. "And Salisbury along with Warwick; and even York's son, the Earl of March."

Margaret drew a soft breath. "But he is just a boy. The King must be very distressed to go to those lengths."

"The Earl of March is seventeen. Young, it's true, but his bow could be the instrument of death to the King, the same as any man's."

Henry Stafford stretched his legs wearily before him, staring into the heat of the fire. "I don't believe it was York's intention to kill the King. He has had ample opportunity to dispose of His Majesty if he so wished."

Margaret stood up and paced around the chamber. "What will happen now?" She stopped near Henry's chair.

He smiled up at her. "York is not a prisoner yet. It may be that the whole thing will blow over, and the King issue a pardon."

He looked at Margaret hesitantly for a moment as if wondering how much he dared say.

"Come, Henry, you don't believe it will end as easily as that, do you? Matters have gone too far for there to be any turning back."

Henry shrugged. "It seems that York may be heading towards London. My father has already set out, to be there before him."

Margaret could imagine the vigorous Duke of Buckingham waiting in readiness to apprehend the unsuspecting Duke of York and she shuddered.

"Will the wars never come to an end? It seems to be all that men think of in these troubled times."

Henry rose to his feet and took her hand in his. "Not all Margaret. You are constantly in my mind. Ever since I first saw you, I've longed to make you my wife."

Margaret tried to draw away, but her hands

were imprisoned in his. She was surprised at the strength contained in Henry's thin frame.

"I have known you less than a year; not very long for me to consider such a serious step as marriage," she smiled to soften her words. "Be patient a little longer Henry, please."

At that moment, the young Earl of Richmond on fat little legs ran into the chamber. His bright hair was tangled on to his shoulders, and his face was flushed with excitement. Behind him came his nurse, bobbing in an agony of embarrassment to Margaret.

"I'm sorry, my lady, he was away so quickly; and I only took my eyes off him for a moment."

Margaret smiled and caught her son in her arms. "You are naughty to treat Joan Hill that way," she reproved. "You know she is new here, and she won't stay long unless you behave yourself."

The Earl chose to disregard his mother's admonition and wriggled away from her to stand before Henry.

"Have you been fighting in the war?" He looked up eagerly with round eyes, and Margaret sighed in exasperation.

"War! That's all I hear from the oldest to the youngest man within these walls."

Henry smiled indulgently. "You have learned to speak very well during my absence, young Earl of Richmond. Your mother tutors you with great care, I can see."

Margaret flushed with pride. She was pleased

with the way her son, not yet three years of age, so quickly learned his lessons.

"Come along, my son," she said with a presence of sternness. "Allow Joan to take you back to the nursery where you belong."

Obediently he took the hand of his nurse, but stopped at the doorway for a moment.

"Are you going to live with us always? I'd like that, because you could teach me to shoot and fight and then I'll be a soldier when I grow up."

Henry Stafford smiled. "I'd like that very much too," he said. "We shall have to ask your mother about it first, I think."

Margaret's colour was high as her son left the chamber. She moved over to the window, knowing in her heart that the time had come to give Henry an answer, one way or another.

He came and stood behind her, placing his hands on her shoulders. "What do you say, Margaret? Will you be my wife?" He turned her slowly to face him, and she sighed gently.

"I have a great affection for you, Henry, and I won't deny that I need the protection of a husband, especially in these troubled times." She paused, uncertain how to continue; and Henry smiled encouragingly at her. "I can never love you the way I loved Edmund," she said quickly. "But I will try to be a good and obedient wife, and if you will accept me on those terms, I will be honoured to marry you."

Henry smiled. "There are many different kinds of love, Margaret, and I am willing to settle for whatever you can offer."

He kissed her gently then and Margaret felt the warm tears on her cheeks as he held her close to his heart.

Owen Tudor hoisted his grandson on to his shoulder and paraded with him around the great hall.

"Your grandfather has returned from the wars my boy, and how heavy you have grown. I can hardly support your weight!"

Margaret smiled indulgently as Jasper came and took both her hands in his.

"It's good to be back at Pembroke for a while. I have heard the news that you are to marry Stafford as soon as arrangements can be made." He smiled at her, a little wistfully. "I am very fond of you, Margaret, perhaps too fond for my own good; but I am happy to know that you will be well cared for. I am a soldier first and last, and women have made up only a small part of my life. I was never the marrying kind and so I am doubly glad that you bore my brother a son. Neither Edmund nor the Tudor name will die while the Earl of Richmond lives. Take good care of him, Margaret."

He kissed her gently on the cheek, and she pressed his hand warmly.

"I love my son more than my own life. You may rest assured that he will be first in my life always."

Owen swung the young Earl down to the

ground before Margaret, and his eyes shone with delight.

"The boy is brave and sturdy. I am proud of him, Margaret. I hope you will always think of Pembroke as your home and his. This is one place where you will be safe."

Margaret nodded. "Thank you, father. I'm glad that you and Jasper approve of my forthcoming marriage." She smiled at Henry drawing him into the group. "But to be practical," she said slowly, "we will need dispensation from the Pope. Henry and I are cousins of the same blood, remember? And I wish everything to be right between us so that we can marry without too much fuss."

"It shall be taken care of, never fear," Jasper smiled at her.

Owen once more swung the young Earl into the air, setting him squealing with laughter, on to his broad shoulder.

Henry took Margaret's hand gently in his, drawing her near to his side, and in that moment, Margaret was happier than she had been since Edmund's death, almost three years ago.

Buckingham was a large man with an air of vitality that commanded attention. He smiled at Margaret and patted Henry on the shoulder with fatherly condescension.

"You are a lucky fellow, my son. You have found a jewel among women in Margaret,

Countess of Richmond." He leaned forward and kissed Margaret on both cheeks. "I have settled lands upon you, my dear, among them the beautiful manors of Hengrave, and Leo's Hall in Westley. This is a mark of my esteem for you, and your kinsmen, the Tudors." He took up his cup. "May the saints bless your union with Henry. I pray you shall both find happiness together."

Margaret tried desperately to feel happy at her own marriage ceremony, but her heavy dress covered with cloth of gold seemed to hold her as if in a trap she could not be free of. She looked across the table at Henry. He, too, seemed strained, and in a moment of sheer panic she wished she had never agreed to become his wife.

Elizabeth was covering the bed with herbs when Margaret at last escaped to her chamber.

"Please remove them!" she said abruptly, as the fresh scents brought back vivid memories of her wedding night with Edmund.

After one startled glance, Elizabeth did as she was bidden, and Margaret sank down into a chair, shaking uncontrollably.

Henry entered the chamber and came to her side at once, his eyes filled with concern.

"What is it, Margaret? Are you ill?" He took her hand and led her gently to the bed. "Come," he whispered in her ear. "We will get into bed so that we can be left alone, then if you wish we shall sit and talk all night long."

Margaret smiled at him gratefully, and soon she was under the cool coverings of the bed.

Henry dismissed the curious ladies who turned lingeringly at the door to watch Margaret as she settled against the bolsters, and then they were alone in the silence of the chamber under the flickering light of the tapers.

"I would not do anything to hurt you, Margaret." Henry took her gently in his arms. She forced herself to smile and affection for his kindly ways rose up inside her.

"You will not hurt me, Henry. I have promised to be a good and obedient wife to you, and I meant every word of it."

With a muffled exclamation, he drew her tightly to him and she closed her eyes, hoping he had not seen the anguish she felt reflected in her expression.

She lay beneath him, dutiful and submissive, telling herself over and over again that she would give Henry her body and her affection because that was all she had to give. She hoped with all her heart he would not notice that she could never give him passion.

The hot sun had turned the sea into gold and against the dazzling water Margaret did not at first notice the straggled line of horsemen picking their way around the coast road.

It was, the young Earl of Richmond warned her, that there were soldiers coming and she turned, startled, her heart in her mouth. As the men drew slowly nearer, she saw the standard of the Tudors billowing out in the stiff breeze; but there was something wrong. The flag was at half-mast.

"Come, my son, we must go down to the steps and greet them. Run and tell Uncle Henry that the soldiers are returning from the war."

It was hot on the steps of the castle, and Margaret's head began to thump as she strained her eyes, trying to see if Owen and Jasper were among the weary band of men.

Henry came to her and placed his arm around her shoulders. His voice was gentle with concern.

"We must be prepared for bad news," he said. "See how they ride with shoulders slumped. It seemed they have been defeated."

"I can see Owen!" Margaret said quickly. "And there is Jasper just behind him. Thank God and all the saints that they have been spared."

Henry was silent, and as the soldiers swung themselves one by one wearily from the saddle, he became white-faced with anxiety.

Owen came directly to him and took his arm. "I have bad news, Stafford," he said quickly. "Your father died bravely in battle, like the great man he was."

Henry nodded as if he had known already and silently followed them into the great hall. Margaret took his hand in an effort to comfort him and he kissed her on the cheek, his eyes full of tears that he would not allow himself to shed.

It was Henry who asked how the defeat came about and Margaret's heart swelled with pride in him. In his grief he was more dignified and suddenly he seemed to grow older.

"The King met the Yorkists at Northampton." Owen flung himself into a chair. "But we were outnumbered, and many a good Lancastrian has been lost to us."

Angrily, Jasper pounded his fist against the stone wall, his bright hair falling across his forehead.

"Richard has called a Parliament in London. He claims the throne as the descendant of Lionel, Duke of Clarence."

Margaret looked at him quickly. "Is his claim to be upheld?" she said fearfully.

Jasper shrugged. "The lords have to admit that the claim has merit, but they are reluctant to pass over my brother, the King. It is my belief that they will set aside the young Prince of Wales, and Richard will take the throne after King Henry's death." He hesitated a moment. "Or after poor Henry finally becomes completely mad."

They retired early to their chamber and Margaret took Henry's hands in her own.

"I know the grief that rests inside you like a stone," she said gently. "I have had my share of it." She wound her arms around him, feeling the tenseness of his muscles beneath her hands. "Come to bed, and let me comfort you," she said softly, and he turned to her, holding her so tightly she could scarcely breathe.

There was a certain joy in giving herself to Henry. She felt that in some small way, by her very closeness, she was helping him to overcome his grief. When he finally fell back on the pillows exhausted, he closed his eyes; and after a few moments, his regular breathing told Margaret that sleep had claimed him.

The Duke of Buckingham had remembered Margaret in his will. She felt tears sting her eyes as his wishes were read out that to his son, Henry, and his daughter, Margaret, Countess of Richmond, should be given the sum of four hundred marks.

Henry did not raise his eyes and Margaret saw with a dart of pity that they were full of tears.

She put out her hand to him. "Your father died as a brave man should. He would not have been content to leave this world lying in a bed."

Henry patted her hand and spoke with an effort. "You are right, Margaret. I know it, but I cannot help grieving for him. He was so alive, so vigorous still."

Young Henry of Richmond pressed himself against Margaret's knee, sensing that all was not right.

"Please take me out shooting at the butts, my Lord Stafford. See how brightly the sun shines over the green. And there's scarcely any wind."

"Don't trouble Uncle Henry just now, my

son," Margaret said and kissed the Earl's shining hair. She would have sent him away, but Stafford got to his feet.

"The boy is right. It is a wonderful day for being outside. I will enjoy a shoot with you. I hope your bow is in good order, Henry Richmond."

Margaret watched them go. Leaning out over the window ledge, foolish tears brimming to her eyes, she saw Stafford's hand rest lightly on the shoulder of her small son.

"They go well together." Elizabeth stopped at Margaret's side, her shrewd eyes missing nothing.

"Yes, they do. I'm happy that my son has a father he can love. He needs a man's hand at his age," Margaret said lightly.

"And have you a husband you can love?" Elizabeth asked, steadily, watching the changing expressions on Margaret's face.

"There will be no man like Edmund," Margaret said firmly, "but Henry Stafford is a fine man, honourable and kindly. I can ask nothing more of life."

Elizabeth handed her some skeins of bright silk and held out the tapestry she had been working on.

"Can you help me with my posy of primroses, Margaret? I seem to have them in a pretty jumble."

Margaret took the tapestry at once and nimbly threaded a needle. As she bent over the work, her brow furrowed in concentration, Elizabeth felt a deep pity in her, that at such a tender age, Margaret was forced to accept life as it was.

Suddenly Margaret, as if aware of her gaze, looked up and read the pity in her eyes.

"Do not waste your sympathy on me, Elizabeth," she said almost gaily. "I have had one all-consuming love in my life and now I'm content to dedicate my life to my son."

She smiled, but in her eyes there was a shadow that nothing would ever chase away.

CHAPTER TWELVE

Pembroke Castle shuddered in the howling winds and driving snows of January, but Henry Tudor, Earl of Richmond, was too busy celebrating his fourth birthday to notice the inclemency of the weather.

Margaret forced herself to smile and join in the fun of the games, but her heart was troubled; she constantly thought of Owen and Jasper, knowing they were again in the midst of battle.

Henry Stafford pressed her arm. "Come, Margaret, you must not brood on matters you can do nothing about. Try to forget outside events, and enjoy the present moment."

Margaret was grateful for his sympathy. "You are right, of course, but the weather is so bitter and Owen is not a young man any longer. I wish they would return home."

"Mother, will you read to me? I'm tired of playing, and my legs ache."

Margaret drew her son to her and rubbed his cold limbs. The dampness of the castle affected her own legs, for they ached intolerably at times.

"I will read to you, but only for a little while. Shall I see you tucked into bed first? You will be warm and snug there."

Elizabeth rose from her seat in the corner. "I will call Joan Hill, Margaret," she said quickly.

"You rest near the fire for a moment. You look exhausted."

Margaret sank back, grateful for the warmth of the blazing logs. "No doubt Owen and Jasper are crouched over some mean fire, resting on the freezing earth," Margaret's voice trembled.

Henry laughed kindly. "They will have entrenched themselves somewhere warm," he said. "You forget they are seasoned soldiers and have learned to survive under all sorts of conditions."

Margaret nodded consideringly, and held her son closer to her. He was almost asleep, and she rested her cheek against his bright hair, feeling love flow through her.

"You are such a comfort."

She stretched her hand out quickly to her husband, wanting to include him in her feeling of contentment, and he smiled lovingly, tracing the curve of her cheek with his finger.

"You are like a madonna," he said softly. "I never cease to thank the saints for giving you to me."

The door opened, sending an icy draught along the floors, so that Margaret's gown billowed round her ankles, as Joan Hill came over to the little group at the fireside. With a neat little curtsey to Margaret, she leaned forward to scoop young Henry into her arms with great efficiency but little warmth.

Margaret studied her for a moment. She was no beauty, but there was about her a certain bearing and dignity that set her apart from the other ladies of the household. Owen had mentioned once that Joan Hill had come from a noble family, but in one way or another their wealth had dwindled, and he had taken her into Pembroke for friendship of her father.

"I promised to read to my son for a little while, Joan." Margaret tried to infuse some warmth into her voice, but it was difficult in the face of the hostile look the girl bestowed on her.

"But the Earl is almost asleep, my lady. Surely you could read to him in the morning."

"I must keep my word to my son. I told him I would read to him tonight, and I will read to him."

Joan swept along the corridor carrying young Henry easily in her arms. Her back was a stiff rod of disapproval and Margaret grimaced ruefully as she followed her into the nursery.

Margaret read softly in French until Henry's eyelids closed like delicate butterflies against his round cheeks. Then she closed the book, holding its weight in both hands.

"I will leave you now, Joan. I apologise if you have been disturbed because of me."

The girl bowed her head but made no reply, and with a sigh Margaret went to the door.

"I hope we are going to be friends, Joan. There is nothing to be gained by being difficult."

The silence of the room was broken only by the gentle breathing of young Henry as he snuggled down into the bedclothes.

Suddenly, there was a commotion in the great

hall and Margaret felt her heart leap to her throat. She put down the heavy book and sped along the dim corridors, oblivious to the icy draughts that came scurrying in through the large, open doors.

"Somerset is here!" Henry hurried towards her. "He has just ridden in fresh from the battle. Pray God it's not bad news."

"My dear cousin, come and warm yourself before the fire. You are soaked and freezing cold."

Margaret tried to stop the pounding of her heart as she led Somerset towards the fire that burnt up brightly under the fresh load of logs.

"Richard of York is dead, and his son with him," Somerset said tiredly. "The Queen was like the she-wolf she is named after!" He shuddered at the memory and took great gulps of the wine Henry Stafford brought him. "When York was dead, the Queen crowned him with a paper diadem and ordered that his head should be placed over the gates of York as a warning to others who would turn against the King."

Margaret quickly made the sign of the cross, feeling ill as she recalled that once Richard had been a guest at her table.

Henry Stafford took her hand in his. "Remember, Margaret, he was an enemy of the crown. It had to end this way."

Somerset pushed himself upright in his chair. "Do not make the mistake of thinking this is the end, Stafford. York's younger son, the Earl of

March, is cut from a different cloth to his father. He will be out for revenge, and he won't care who falls under his axe."

Margaret shuddered. "You must rest, cousin. I will have warmers put into a bed for you lest you catch cold." She turned to see that Joan Hill was standing behind her watching Somerset intently. "Ah, Joan, will you go to the servants for me, so that a bed may be prepared?"

Joan Hill inclined her head. "I will see to it personally, my lady," she said graciously, and Margaret lifted her eyebrows in surprise.

"She must have taken a liking to you, Somerset," Margaret smiled at him. "She is not usually so accommodating."

He shook his head. "I had not noticed her. A sure sign that I am mortally weary!" Henry Stafford helped him to rise. "Goodnight, cousin Margaret. Oh! I am forgetting a most important message I was bidden to hand you!"

He smiled and reached inside his doublet, handing Margaret a mud-bespattered letter. She took it, her hands trembling, and opened it out carefully, taking only a few moments to read the few scrawled words.

"Owen and Jasper are well and are marching towards the Welsh border," she said in delight. "That means they should be home before too long. Thanks be to God and all the saints."

Somerset shook his head. "Don't harbour false hopes, Margaret. This battle is not done yet."

Suddenly, in spite of the huge fire, Margaret was cold.

The dark months of winter moved miserably on and Margaret became nervous at the ominous lack of news. She spent much of her time in prayer, lighting candles in the cold winter light of dawn, expecting that each day would bring some sign that the war had come to an end.

Her son was a constant source of delight to her, and these days, Joan Hill was far more willing to allow her charge his freedom. It wasn't until the girl fell into a swoon in Margaret's presence that she noticed how pale and listless Joan had become.

"I feel so guilty," she said to Elizabeth. "Perhaps I have been placing too much on the girl's shoulders."

"Nonsense!" Elizabeth's voice was brisk. "She's missing her lover, that is all."

"Her lover? What on earth do you mean?" Margaret was quite bewildered at the turn the conversation had taken and Elizabeth looked at her in amazement.

"Surely you knew that she had taken a liking to your cousin, the Duke of Somerset?" She shrugged her shoulders. "I don't blame her. He's a handsome young man and going off to war again. It was all quite romantic really."

Margaret shook her head. "You mean that Joan Hill bedded with my cousin?" Her colour was high as she stared at Elizabeth in consternation.

"Well, yes, I thought you knew about it. I thought the whole of Pembroke knew about it. It was no secret."

Thoughtfully Margaret walked across the chamber to stare out at the bleak winter landscape.

"I only hope there is not going to be a child. It would ruin poor Joan's life."

The idea was obviously a new one to Elizabeth. "That would bring Miss High-and-Mighty down a station or two," she said with amusement. "She is far too superior, with her airs and graces."

Margaret tutted a little. "You should be more charitable. It would be an awful situation to find yourself in."

Elizabeth was unrepentant. "She should have thought of that before she climbed beneath the sheets. Now she has to pay for her fun."

Margaret turned away from the window. "I'd better talk to her right away," she said. "Please ask her to come to see me if she is feeling better. And Elizabeth, on no account say a word to her about any of this."

"I'll leave everything to you, Margaret. The uppity little creature would never confide in me, anyway."

Joan was dressed unbecomingly in a grey gown. Above the neckline of black velvet, her skin seemed sallow and there were purple shadows underneath her eyes.

"Joan, please sit down." Margaret made an effort to speak lightly. "I hope you are feeling a little better now."

The girl inclined her head, but there was a sullen look about her mouth.

Margaret tried again to communicate a feeling of sympathy and friendship.

"Have you anything that troubles you, Joan? Anything you may like to talk to me about?"

The girl shook her head, and Margaret decided it would be better to come straight to the point.

"Is it true that you are fond of my cousin, the Duke of Somerset?"

Colour raced into the girl's cheeks and suddenly, to Margaret's consternation, she burst into tears.

"Please, Joan, try not to upset yourself. It won't mend matters, it will only make you feel ill again." She patted her arm awkwardly. "I'm trying to help you. Please think of me as a friend."

"I'm sure I'm with child, my lady." Joan hid her face in her kerchief. "It is two months now since I was properly well."

Margaret leaned forward. "Don't cry. Let us think things out calmly and sensibly."

She paused, giving Joan time to compose herself, wondering what her cousin, the Duke of Somerset, would say when he returned from the war to find himself a father.

"What makes you think you are with child?" Margaret said at last. "Have you any definite symptoms?"

Joan gulped a little and stopped crying, though she still avoided Margaret's eyes.

"I have had a feeling of nausea in the mornings, my lady, and my breasts feel full and heavy. I'm certain I'm with child; there can be no doubt about it."

"Well don't worry, you will be well looked after. When the baby comes, something will be arranged."

Margaret did not quite know what she could do. No doubt Owen Tudor would have arranged a speedy marriage if he'd been at home, but Margaret hardly knew anyone from the surrounding countryside, and at any rate all the men of marriageable age were probably at war.

"From now on, you are excused duties, of course," she said soothingly. "It would be best if you stayed in your room and rested as much as possible."

Suddenly Joan got to her feet. "I don't want a child!" she said hysterically. "I hate the thought of it growing within me. And as for tending a mewling infant, the idea sickens me."

Margaret pressed her hands against her skirts, trying to be calm. "You should have thought of that before you consented to be in Somerset's bed," she said coldly, unable to understand a woman who felt that way about her own child.

"But my lady, the Duke seduced me. I told

him I was virtuous, and he took no notice of my protestations."

Margaret clasped her hands together, fighting for control.

"Are you trying to say that Somerset raped you? Did he force his way into your room?"

Joan looked down at her hands a little shame-faced. "Well, no. I went to his room, but I only wanted to be kind, because he had come from the wars, my lady."

"Go to your room, now." Margaret turned away, trying to hide her anger. "I will let you know what I have decided when I have had time to think."

Joan bobbed a curtsey, her eyes sullen behind the reddened lids. "Very well, my lady. I know you'll do what is best for me and your cousin's child."

Margaret went to the window and stared out unseeingly. The war had a great deal to answer for and sometimes it seemed it would never be over and done with.

Sighing, she leaned her hands on the sill and for some unaccountable reason felt loneliness rise inside her like a recurring sickness she could not throw off. She closed her eyes and saw in her mind's eye a picture of Edmund, his young face smiling and his hair alive and bright, falling to his shoulders. Tears came then and alone in the darkened room, she wept for something — some spirit of laughter and love that had gone from her life for ever.

CHAPTER THIRTEEN

Clusters of snowdrops forced their way through the hard ground, even though the mountains still wore their winter mantle of snow. The February days were bright and crisp bringing with them the hope that the battles would soon be ended.

Margaret often sat under the big window facing the path that wound its way over the hills, hoping that one day soon she would see Owen's army returning with the Tudor standard flying high.

"Margaret, I wish you would rest sometimes." Henry came and sat beside her, his face a picture of concern. "You will strain your eyes doing all that needlework. Why don't you just sit before the fire and chatter to the ladies? I'm sure you spend too much time alone."

She smiled at him warmly, stretching her fingers to exercise them. "You are right as usual, Henry," she said. "My hands are quite cramped." She folded her tapestry, tucking the ends of silk carefully into the folds of the cloth. "I will return to it tomorrow when the light is stronger."

"You are worrying about your kinsmen. I know you too well by now for you to hide your feelings from me." He put his hand over hers. "They will return before long. Try not to think about it. You are only tormenting yourself."

Margaret sighed. "I worry about them both, but mainly about Owen. He is an old man and should not be out in the cold of winter camping on the frozen earth." She looked into his face. "I have a feeling deep inside me that all is not well with them. I may be foolish, but I cannot shake the fear away."

Henry called gently to Elizabeth. "Bring some wine. I think the Lady Margaret is in the throes of a chill."

Elizabeth came at once, clucking her tongue and laying a hand on Margaret's brow.

"I do believe you are feverish, Margaret. Why not go to your room and I will bring you something hot to make you sleep?"

"All right," Margaret shrugged. "If it will make you both happy, then I will go to bed."

She suddenly felt as if she wanted nothing more than to snuggle under warm sheets. Perhaps Henry was right and she had caught a chill.

Margaret brought a taper near the bed and sat for a moment with a gospel open on her knee, reading in silence until Elizabeth bustled into the chamber, carrying a potion of boiled herbs. When she was settled into bed, Elizabeth drew a stool up beside her and waited to take the empty cup.

"What is to be done about Joan Hill, Margaret?" she said impatiently. "She sits around issuing orders to everyone else since you relieved her of her duties. Though I must say the young Earl of Richmond is happier without her long face around the nurseries."

Margaret could not help smiling. "Try to have some sympathy, Elizabeth. The girl is going through a difficult time, though I agree she is a prickly person to talk to."

Elizabeth snorted inelegantly. "She is revelling in all the attention, Margaret. She is thrilled that everyone knows she has been with a man."

"Oh, surely not!" Margaret said, sinking back on to the bolster. "No one else knows about her condition except for us."

"Bless you, Margaret, you are too innocent. There is talk of nothing else. Even the servants are gossiping about it. The winter is long and at least Joan Hill has provided us all with a diversion."

Margaret felt a pleasant sleepiness steal over her, but shook her head feeling she should remonstrate with Elizabeth.

"The fact is my cousin was wrong to do such a thing. I will have to see that she does not suffer too much by it."

"She will never let you forget that Somerset is the father of her bastard," Elizabeth said quickly. "She intends to get the utmost out of the situation, so that far from suffering from it, she will benefit. She does not seem to care about the disgrace."

Margaret held her hand up tiredly. "I would like to sleep now, Elizabeth. Be kind to the girl, for my sake if not for hers."

Elizabeth rose and tucked the covers more

snugly around Margaret's shoulder.

"Too good for this world, that's what you are! But I will try to be charitable, if it will make you feel any better."

She went then and Margaret thankfully closed her eyes feeling as if she was just recovering from a very long illness.

The snow on the mountain was beginning to melt when Margaret saw a small crowd of riders come over the mountain road. Ignoring the colcl, she flung open the window and leaned out, straining to see if any standard was flying. She saw none — just a tired line of horsemen picking their way over the hard track towards the castle.

"Henry!" she called anxiously. "Someone is coming towards the yard. I can't see who it can be."

Henry took her hand and leaned over her. "I too saw them. It is your cousin, the Duke of Somerset, and some of his men."

Margaret felt fear tug at her heart. "It is bad news, Henry, I know it."

He pressed her hand gently. "Be calm, Margaret. It probably isn't as bad as you think." He released her and went to the door, flinging it wide to welcome the Duke.

He came to Margaret, his young face haggard. "I have ill news. I'm sorry to be the one to have to tell you."

Margaret fingered the cross at her throat, the colour draining from her cheeks.

"Owen and Jasper? Are they dead?" She felt as if she were in a bad dream and shortly she would wake from it, but Somerset was speaking again.

"Jasper managed to escape from the field, dressed as a monk. And I am sure he got well away from Mortimers Cross." He looked down at his hands that shook with weariness. "Owen was executed after the battle. He died bravely, with Queen Catherine's name on his lips."

Margaret gave a little cry, and Henry took her hands in his.

"Have some wine, Margaret, it will make you feel better." He held the cup to her lips and she took a drink, scarcely knowing what she was doing.

"Tell me all of it, Somerset. I must know," she said, forcing herself to be calm.

He hesitated for a moment, and Henry nodded to him to continue.

"When it was done, an old crone came along. No one knows from where, and washed the blood from Owen Tudor's face and combed his hair and set four candles around him to ward off evil spirits. It was an unearthly sight and every soldier there trembled and prayed to the saints to protect them."

"How could anyone execute a fine gentleman of Owen's years?" Margaret said distractedly. "It does not bear thinking about."

Somerset shrugged his broad shoulders. "The Earl of March is young, about your age, Margaret. He seeks revenge for what Queen

Margaret did to his father, the Duke of York. War makes barbarians of us all."

"And what of the Queen?" Henry asked. "Did she escape capture?"

Somerset nodded. "She marched south with the Prince of Wales to face Warwick, and she had a resounding victory over him." He paused thoughtfully. "It all rests on one thing. Who will reach London first, the Queen or the Earl of March?"

For a moment there was silence as each one present tried to imagine young Edward ruling England.

"It is not likely that it will come to that," Somerset said reassuringly. "The Queen has worked miracles so far. Let us pray she continues to do so."

Margaret forced herself to remember that her cousin had ridden long and hard. "You must eat, Somerset, and then rest. You must be tired beyond endurance."

He took her hand gratefully. "Margaret, you have my deepest sympathy in your loss. I know how much Owen Tudor had come to mean to you."

She inclined her head without answering. There was nothing to say. Some things went too deep for any words.

Something had awakened Margaret. She sat up in her bed and tried to identify the sound. It was like someone crying out loud along the long corridors of the castle. She shivered and rushed into Henry's arms as he appeared from the other chamber.

"What on earth is going on?" she said sleepily. "Who is making that awful caterwauling?"

Together they moved to the door and Henry looked outside, holding Margaret back with one hand.

"Let me see what is happening," he said firmly. "You wait here."

Reluctantly Margaret stopped near the door, wishing she had more tapers lit to dispel some of the shadows.

Henry quickly returned, his colour high. "It is Joan Hill. She is at Somerset's door talking a great deal of nonsense if you ask me."

Margaret sighed. "Is that all? Leave this to me, Henry. I will settle the matter. She is a foolish girl."

Somerset was standing at the door of his chamber, red to his ears with embarrassment.

"Cousin, come and sort this out," he appealed. "I am quite bewildered by the tirade this young lady has subjected me to."

Margaret drew Somerset back into his chamber indicating that Joan Hill should come too, and closed the door in the faces of the curious ladies gathered outside in the corridor.

"Now what do you mean by this stupidity, Joan? Couldn't your business wait until a respectable hour of the morning?"

Margaret was so angry she could hardly speak. She clenched her hands to her side in an effort to stop them trembling.

Joan had the grace to look ashamed. "I'm sorry, my lady, but the Duke refused to open his door to me."

"Refused?" Somerset was indignant. "I did no such thing! I was so dead tired I failed to hear anyone knock; that is the truth of the matter."

Margaret held up her hand for silence as Joan began to speak again. "Do you realise that my cousin is straight returned from the field of battle, Joan? You could at least have allowed him one night's rest before you told him your plight."

Somerset shook his head in exasperation. "I wish someone would tell me what this is all about," he said abruptly.

"I am to have your child, sir," Joan said hotly. "I need your help, and you won't even listen to me."

Margaret saw the shock on her cousin's young face as he digested the information.

"Is this true?" he said, and turned to Margaret for confirmation.

"It is true, but nothing can be gained by everyone becoming hysterical, especially at this time of night." She moved purposefully to the door. "Come, Joan, we will talk this over calmly and sensibly in the morning."

Reluctantly Joan Hill followed her to the door. She turned back for a moment to look at Somerset.

"I will see you in the morning, my lord?" Her voice was pleading and Somerset nodded.

"Naturally I will take responsibility for the child, but it would be better to allow matters to rest there for tonight. I promise I will speak to you tomorrow."

Margaret sent Joan to her bed and turned back into the room. "There is not a great deal you can do for the girl, Somerset, except to make adequate provision for the child." She brushed back a tendril of hair from her forehead. "I will try to arrange a match for her. I'm sure that is what Owen would have done."

Her voice broke and tears trembled on her lashes. Somerset came towards her and held her gently in his arms for a moment.

"I'm sorry to bring you more trouble at such a time. I had no idea that I'd made the girl with child."

Margaret shook her head and strove for composure. "I understand better than you think. I don't blame you for taking what was so readily offered." She moved away from him. "Try to sleep now. We will think of the best way to deal with this when we are all well rested. I don't know what the girl was thinking about disturbing everyone at this unearthly hour."

An impish smile sped across Somerset's face. "It might have been love for me," he said quickly, "though more likely it was love for my purse that inspired her."

Margaret shook her head reprovingly. "There doesn't seem to be much sleep left in you, cousin. I'd advise you to take a cold wash and then get back into bed — your own bed!"

She let herself out of the room and closed the door quietly behind her, stifling a yawn. Perhaps she would be able to fall asleep straight away. She was so tired she could hardly stand. But when she returned to her own chamber, Henry was waiting there, his arms open wide to receive her.

CHAPTER FOURTEEN

Shrill screams echoed around the chamber where Joan Hill lay labouring to give birth to her child. Candles flickered like live wraiths against the tapestries, and in the long corridors sudden gusts of wild played eerie tunes.

Margaret stood at the bedside of the stricken girl, bathing her feverish brow with cool scented water. She looked across enquiringly at the midwife, knowing that no woman on earth could hold out against such pain indefinitely.

The nurse shook her head. "The way things are going now, I can't promise that the lady or the child will live to see morning," she whispered.

"Can nothing be done to help?" Margaret said anxiously. "It is hard to stand aside and watch such suffering."

"I can give her some herbs that will help her to sleep; that is all," the midwife said quietly. "I will rest now, my lady, by your leave. There is nothing can be done for an hour or two."

"I will sit with her," Margaret said at once. "I will call you if anything happens."

The potion quietened Joan for the moment and Margaret sat down, her hand resting on the empty crib, that had been her son's. It seemed fitting that Somerset's child should lie in it, even though he would be born on the wrong side of the blanket.

She dozed a little and the wind outside seemed to become one with the moaning of the girl on the bed. Suddenly she was wide awake. Joan Hill was leaning up on her elbow, her long hair tangled around her face, her hands clutching her full stomach.

"My son is about to be born. Will you bring help for me, my lady?"

Margaret called out sharply to the midwife and returned to the bedside.

"Try to reserve your strength, Joan. The midwife is coming. You will be in good hands."

Joan grimaced with pain. "I want my child to live. About myself it doesn't seem to matter any longer."

Margaret hushed her. "Don't talk like that. Everything that can be done will be done, I promise you."

The midwife made herself busy, her hands deft and gentle, and soon she had drawn the child into the world.

"A lusty boy!" she said triumphantly as loud cries echoed around the chamber. "See how strong he is?"

Joan made an effort to smile as she lay back, white and exhausted against the bolster.

"I wish him to be called Charles," she said thinly, her lips trembling and bloodless. "Promise he will be brought up like a gentleman."

Margaret bent over her, admiring the courage

that Joan had shown throughout her long ordeal.

"He will be brought up as well as my own son. He is my kin and will be treated as such."

For a long moment Joan regarded her steadily. "I know you are faithful to your word, and I am happy." A small sigh escaped her lips and her eyes slowly closed.

Anxiously Margaret turned to the midwife. "Is there nothing to be done?"

The midwife shook her head slowly. "It is in God's hands now, my lady. I can do no more."

Cold winds were lashing the countryside and through them Edward, Earl of March, won the race to London. The people, sick to their souls of war, proclaimed him King, and he lost no time in rallying men to his banner.

The soldiers of the south were weary of the barbaric attacks made on them by the Queen's rough northerners, and willingly followed Edward in his pursuit of the French Margaret of Anjou.

Hidden away behind the stout walls of Pembroke Castle. Margaret knew nothing of the direction the war had taken. She had been present at the death of Joan Hill and had taken the tiny newborn child in her arms, promising before all the saints that she would care for him as if he there her own.

The Earl of Richmond had become a sturdy, self-sufficient boy with a kindly affection for the baby, a feeling which Margaret fostered, knowing that the time might come when the two children would find mutual benefit in such a friendship.

It wasn't until the icy grip of winter had loosened its hold that a rider made his way over the winding path towards the castle. Margaret met him at the door, eager for news, and found a young priest with deeply etched lines of fatigue mapping his face.

"The news is bad, my lady," he said wearily as she drew him near to the blazing logs. "The armies met at Towton and there was such slaughter as I've never seen before. It was said that thirty-eight thousand dead lay scattered about the field." He paused for a moment, his eyes clouded with memory. "The Queen pressed on bravely, but she was defeated once more at Hexam, and was forced to flee to France."

Margaret's lips were dry. "What of the King?" she asked, a sudden fear tightening around her heart.

"He is taken to the Tower, my lady. It appears that his sickness has come upon him again."

He swayed a little and Margaret led him to a chair. "I will see that you have food and drink and a good bed for as long as you need it," she said quietly. "I thank you for coming to tell me all this."

He held up his hand. "My lady, there is more bad news for you to bear, I fear. Please try to be calm, I beg you."

"What is it?" Margaret clasped her hands

tightly together, feeling faint with apprehension.

The priest coughed a little, seeking for a palatable way to break the news. "Your cousin, young Somerset — he fell in battle, my lady. And Lord Welles, too. They fought bravely, you may be assured of that."

Margaret closed her eyes; how many more of her kinsmen would die at the sword of Edward, Earl of March, now King of England?

She began to pray for strength while in her mind the thought lay like a black bat that it was only a matter of time before Edward moved against her son.

"My lady, there are soldiers moving towards the castle!" Elizabeth was almost hysterical in her fear and Margaret put a calming hand around her waist.

"It may be that the remnants of the Lancastrian army have found their way home," she said soothingly, though it was not at all a likely prospect. "Go and call my husband, just in case."

Anxiously, she went to look from the tower and saw the unfamiliar standard fluttering in the breeze. Her heart contracted with fear and she hurried to the great hall to await the arrival of the soldiers, joined immediately by Henry.

The retinue came to a standstill and a tall, kindly-looking man bowed before her, nodding respectfully towards Henry Stafford.

"I am William, Lord Herbert. I have come to tell you that your young son, the Earl of

Richmond, and his uncle, Jasper Tudor, have been attainted. The honour of the title Earl of Pembroke now rests with me and the King, Edward the Fourth, has instructed me to take your son as my ward."

Henry placed a hand on his sword and stepped forward a pace, but Margaret restrained him.

"Enter Pembroke Castle if you must, but please leave me my son," she said brokenly; and Lord Herbert turned his head, avoiding her eyes.

"I cannot grant your request, my lady. Do not worry about your son. My wife and I will care for him as if he were our own child." He walked past her into the great hall. "It may even be possible to arrange an alliance between your son and my daughter, Maud. I will at least give the matter some thought."

"Never!" So suddenly did she speak that Lord Herbert stared at her in surprise. Margaret drew herself up to her full height. "You may take him from me, but I will never consent to him marrying into a Yorkist family, my lord."

Lord Herbert shrugged. "I am sorry to hear that. But the time may come when you will change your views. Yorkists are not come from the devil, you know. We are men of flesh and blood, just like Lancastrians."

Margaret was silent and Lord Herbert despatched his men to bring out the Earl.

Henry put his arm around her to steady her. "Try to be brave, Margaret," he said softly. "The King may still return to his senses, and then this Edward will be forced to relinquish the throne."

Henry Richmond, Earl of Pembroke, clattered down the stairs and crossed the room in quick short steps to his mother's side.

"Is it true that I am to go with these men, mother?" he asked, staring in suspicion at Lord Herbert.

Margaret almost choked on her tears, but she took her son in her arms and fondled his bright hair.

"What harm could a seven-year-old boy do to the new King, my lord?" she said pleadingly, but Herbert turned his face away in silence. "Go with them for now, my son." She held him close once more. "It won't be for long. And Lord Herbert is a good man. See that you continue with your studies."

She watched as they took him outside and set him on a horse and then as they rode away across the rugged path, she turned into Henry's arms and wept.

"Mother, how good it is to see you again!" Margaret drew the Duchess of Somerset into the warmth of the chamber and handed her a glass of wine.

"You haven't changed a bit. You look just as fresh and young as I've always remembered you."

She looked well in her black garments of widowhood, Margaret decided, though there were new lines etched at the corners of her mother's eyes and some grey among the fair hairs curling from under the velvet headdress.

"My dear Margaret," the Duchess sighed, "it seems only the other day you were a little child sitting on Leo's knee and now he's gone from me for ever."

"I was distressed to hear of his death at Towton, mother. I was very fond of him, you know that."

The Duchess put away her lace kerchief. "We have both suffered, Margaret, but we must be strong. We both have our sons to comfort us."

Margaret looked down at her hands, fighting to control the tears that brimmed into her eyes. "I wish my son was with me. It is hard to think of him being brought up by another woman, however kindly she might be."

The Duchess leaned forward and patted her hand. "He is alive and well, Margaret. It is a great deal to be thankful for in such times." She drank a little of her wine and regarded Margaret steadily, her eyes betraying her curiosity. "What is this I hear about you bringing up a Somerset bastard?"

"Mother, please don't speak so loudly," Margaret said quickly. "Someone might hear you. I promised I would bring him up as if he were my own child, and I intend to do just that."

"Very commendable," the Duchess said drily, "but there can be no profit in it for you."

"I do not look for profit," Margaret said

mildly. "He is a fine boy, robust and healthy, the very image of Somerset. I have grown to love him."

"You must show him to me," the Duchess said comfortably. "You have made me eager to see him for myself." Before Margaret could frame an answer, her mother was on a new train of thought. "Margaret, I have come to the conclusion that we should both join the fraternity of the Abbey of Croyland. I have been approached on the matter and I view the idea with favour."

"It would be a great honour, mother," Margaret said, and patiently waited for her mother to explain.

The Duchess slowly took a sip of her wine before continuing.

"You will, of course, be heiress to the manor of Deeping, which is near Croyland. I am merely holding it in dower for you from your father's estates." She smiled. "The abbot would be grateful if you were to pass on some, or indeed all, of the land to them, and you never know when you will need help or sanctuary in these troubled times."

"May we never be in need of sanctuary, mother," Margaret said quickly. "But no doubt you are wise to think of such things."

Her mother put down her glass. "Now, that is settled, I would like to go to my room and rest for a time. The journey took longer than I thought. Later, perhaps, you could show me Somerset's boy. Was it Charles you named him?"

Margaret helped her mother to her feet. "Joan Hill asked that he should be named Charles. Naturally, I deferred to her wishes."

"Naturally," the Duchess said drily, "though I should have been inclined to choose some other name. Charles is so ordinary. No, do not come with me. I can find my room alone. I'm not infirm yet."

The moment her mother was out of sight, Henry joined Margaret near the fire.

"Did you find a great deal to talk about?" he smiled. "The conversation seemed a bit one-sided to me, though I may have been mistaken."

"My mother is a great one for holding forth," Margaret said good-naturedly. "But she usually talks a great deal of sense."

Henry nodded. "She is a fine woman, and bears her grief well. Losing Lord Welles must have been a great shock."

Margaret stared into the glowing fire, feeling the familiar ache that came whenever she thought of her son.

"These wars between the Houses of Lancaster and York have a great deal to answer for," she said wearily. "We have lost some of the finest men in England into the greedy hands of war."

"It has to end," Henry said cheerfully, "and then you will have your son restored to you."

"That is my prayer every night when I go to my bed, and every morning when I open my eyes."

Henry sat beside her and carefully brushed

away her tears. "Your prayers will be answered, Margaret, I feel sure of it. One day soon King Henry will be restored to his rightful place and Edward, the usurper, will be overthrown. As for your son, the Earl of Richmond, there is a great future ahead for him. I feel it deep within me and you will be there to share his triumph."

Margaret attempted to smile through her tears, holding out her hands to Henry. "I do not know what I would have done throughout all this if I hadn't been blessed with you to comfort and support me. You are so good and kind. I sometimes feel I'm not worthy of you."

"What nonsense!" Henry smiled warmly and kissed Margaret's fingers. "I would not have any other woman in the whole of the kingdom, not even the Queen herself." He pinched her cheek playfully. "Enough of this melancholy talk. Let us go up to the nurseries and see little Charles."

Elizabeth was sitting beside the crib talking foolishness to the child. It seemed that everyone had taken him to their hearts because of the tragic circumstances that had made him an orphan in his infancy.

Margaret leaned over to smile down at Charles and he immediately lifted his arms to her, begging her with round eyes to lift him up in her arms.

"You will spoil him," Elizabeth said reprovingly, but she smiled as Margaret handed the child to Henry.

"Impossible!" Margaret said. "He has such a

sweet nature that nothing could spoil him."

Elizabeth got to her feet. "Well, I promised to help your mother, the Duchess, settle into her chamber. I must keep my word, or I'll feel the sharp edge of her tongue.

"We had such high hopes she and I; mine, alas, came to naught. I have neither husband nor child to call my own."

Margaret looked at her with surprise. She had forgotten that Elizabeth had been friends with her mother in the old days at Bletsoe.

"I never realised you wanted to marry," she said softly. "I suppose I selfishly imagined that this life here with us was what you wished from life."

Elizabeth clucked her tongue. "Don't you take any notice of my ramblings. It comes over me every now and then that life has passed me by, especially when I think back at times gone and over with." She walked to the door. "Your mother and I will talk ourselves dry as dust, so if you don't mind I'll take some wine along to her chamber with me."

"Of course," Margaret said quickly, "have the servants bring you anything you like."

Margaret stood thoughtful and silent for a moment after Elizabeth had left the room, re-alising how much she had taken the older woman for granted.

"What's on your mind?" Henry came and stood beside her holding Charles gently in the crook of his arm.

She smiled warmly at him. He looked so handsome and paternal with the baby asleep against him that tears came to her eyes.

"I'm just reminding myself how fortunate I am," she said quietly, and standing on tiptoe, she gently kissed his cheek.

CHAPTER FIFTEEN

The great chamber thronged with people. Jewels flashed on rich velvets of red and purple as the ladies of the Court attempted to outshine each other in brilliance.

As Margaret moved forward with her son, the Earl of Richmond, at her side, the press of people and the intensity of the noise was almost too much for her.

"Come, my son; stay with me while I sit in this alcove for a moment." She settled herself on the window seat, fanning herself with her lace kerchief. "It has all been too much for me," she said, smiling. "King Henry restored to his throne and best of all, Jasper bringing you back to me." She pressed his arm and Henry returned her smile a little self-consciously.

He had grown tall, and there was already the promise of broadness to his shoulders. Margaret felt a pang of regret that she had not been allowed to witness his transformation from a child into a young man of fourteen years.

"Time flies so quickly." She uttered her thoughts out loud and the Earl of Richmond smiled down at her with pride.

"In that blue gown you look young enough to be my sister. You are more beautiful even than I had remembered you."

Margaret's laugh held a trace of tears. "I see

you have your father's pretty tongue when it comes to women." She patted the seat beside her and obediently, Henry came to her side.

"In spite of everything that has happened, mother, I was grieved to see Lord Herbert taken away from his home and killed by rebels. He was a good man and like a father to me."

Margaret longed to hold her son close and comfort him, to drive away the desolation in his voice.

"Times are hard, my son. There are bitter lessons to be learned by all of us."

Henry looked thoughtful. "Uncle Jasper talked about taking me to France if things didn't work out well for the King."

"Hush, my son." Margaret looked around fearfully, but no one seemed to be listening to the conversation. "It is dangerous to speak so. Be careful in everything you say."

Henry lowered his voice to a whisper. "Do you think Edward has a chance of returning, mother? Why, Warwick has turned against him and has placed King Henry once more on the throne. Surely Warwick is the most powerful man in the kingdom."

Margaret's eyes grew dark. "I have seen other men, more powerful even than Warwick, dashed from power. And see how frail the King has become. He is like an old man, not knowing or caring what will happen to him."

Henry Richmond stood at full stretch to look at the King. He was indeed so gaunt as to appear like a skull beneath his fine crown. At his side sat his Queen, her face filled with almost hysterical delight because once more she held England in her greedy grasp.

"So there you are!" Jasper Tudor threw back his head and laughed. "I saw your red head pop up behind the crowd like a lighted taper, Henry. There was no mistaking you." He took Margaret's hand in his. "You must pay your respects to the King," he said, "though it may well be that he does not remember you. He is not exactly lucid at this moment."

Jasper's strong shoulders soon cleared a pathway to the throne.

"Sire," he bowed low to the King. "This boy is my brother Edmund's son, Henry Richmond."

For a moment, the King's eyes seemed to be anywhere but on the boy standing before him. Then his vision cleared and he stretched out his thin hand.

"Come here, Henry Richmond, I would see you more clearly."

Silence spread through the chamber like ripples in a pool. Everyone seemed to be waiting for the King to speak.

"England's hope," he said. "I see a crown glitter on your head, my son. You will bring order to my poor war-torn land."

The Queen tried to distract him by pulling at his arm, but the King took no notice of her.

"You are the last hope of the House of Lancaster, I know you will carry the burden of kingship with courage and wisdom."

The Queen could be silent no longer. "He is bewildered!" She appealed to those nearest her for confirmation, but no one spoke. "He must be imagining that this boy is our own son. There can be no other explanation."

Her words were greeted with silence. Everyone had heard the King call the boy by name. There could be no misunderstanding.

The Queen's colour rose. "Let there be music!" She tapped her foot angrily and immediately the musicians were galvanised into action.

The King turned to Jasper. "Take good care of this sprig of Lancaster," he said, his voice rising above the music. "He will join the red rose to the white, and will bring peace to the realm."

Jasper bowed and Margaret pulled at her son's sleeve, drawing him away from the throne.

"The King's words are strange, Henry, because an old woman from the streets of London prophesied the same thing many years ago." She shook her head. "I don't understand how you could join such bitter enemies as Lancaster and York. It is beyond my comprehension."

Henry pressed her arm. "The King is not himself today, mother."

Margaret became aware that some of the courtiers were looking at her curiously. "You are right of course, Henry," she said quickly. "Off you go and dance with some pleasant girl of your own age. I am making you old before your time, with my silly talk."

185

Jasper touched her arm. "Come, let us try to find a quiet chamber somewhere away from the crowd. I would like to talk to you privately."

He led her away from the hall and Margaret sighed with relief.

"The atmosphere in there was oppressive," she said lightly. "I think I have been away from Court too long. I have grown accustomed to some peace and quiet."

Jasper took her hand in his. "Now that the King has named Henry as the last hope of Lancaster, we must be doubly careful with him. A sharp knife on a dark night would end all that."

Margaret shuddered. "What can be done?" Her voice trembled with fear for her son.

"Don't worry, I have a ship waiting at the ready," Jasper said quietly. "If there is any sign of Edward returning to do battle, I will take young Henry across to France."

Margaret touched the cross at her throat. "Do you think it a likely event that Edward will take the throne once more?"

Jasper nodded. "It is a certainty! His brother-in-law, Charles of Burgundy, will help him gather an army, and remember, Edward is very popular with the people of England." He smiled impishly. "They love him for his indulgences. It shows he is a man like everyone else. He's had more women even than I have had!"

Margaret could not help smiling, remembering that Jasper Tudor had even numbered the Queen among his conquests. She studied him for a moment, seeing the resemblance between him and her son; both had inherited the strong red hair and the proud bearing of Owen Tudor. She sighed, thinking of dead husband Edmund. He too had worn the handsome looks of the Tudor family.

"We had better return to the great hall." Jasper took her arm. "We will mingle with the courtiers and no one will pay any attention to us."

He laughed, well aware that they would be the focus of attention. His amorous nature was no secret and Margaret, Countess of Richmond, was an attractive woman. Her skin flawless and pale, her hair sleek beneath the tall headdress of black lace.

Margaret returned with Jasper to the comparative seclusion of the window seat.

"What of Edward's wife? What is her situation now that he has fled the country?" She looked up at Jasper with genuine concern and he wondered at her kindness.

"You are generous to spare her even so much as a thought, my dear Margaret," he said drily. "I doubt if she will be so considerate of you."

"I cannot help that," Margaret said gently. "I am curious about her and her little girls."

"They are quite safe, so do not worry your pretty little head about them," Jasper smiled. "They have gone into sanctuary at Westminster. It is rumoured that Elizabeth is once more with child. If she bears a son, it will make the Yorkists even stronger."

"Poor lady," Margaret said impulsively. "To be with child and locked away in such agony of uncertainty. It must be almost more than she can bear."

"Don't feel too sorry for her," Jasper said. "Elizabeth Woodville still sees herself as Queen of England. Still, in the event of Edward returning to the throne, we could always consider a marriage between his eldest daughter and your son."

Margaret gasped. "Oh, but he is so young to think of marriage!"

Jasper looked at her with his eyebrows raised. "You bore him when you were just thirteen, are you forgetting?"

The colour came into Margaret's cheeks. "I will never forget my marriage to Edmund. Brief as it was, it was the happiest time of my life." She frowned. "But it is different now. Henry's future must be carefully mapped out. There is so much at stake."

"I won't argue with that, my dear Margaret, but think of it; if your son were to marry the daughter of Edward the Fourth, it would be a true union of the white rose and the red."

Margaret looked up at him sharply. "Could that be what King Henry had in mind?"

Jasper shrugged. "No one can tell what he thinks, poor demented man. It was a cruelty to bring him out from the Tower at all. I'm sure he would much rather die in peace."

Margaret made the sign of the cross. "Jasper,

do not talk like that!"

He rose to his feet. "It would be better for me to take my leave of you now. We don't want too many courtiers speculating about our friendship. There are too many ready to entertain suspicions for us to be careless."

He bent formally over her hand and pushed his way through the throng of people. A short while later, Margaret saw his bright hair as he bent over the Queen. She was smiling, her small pointed teeth overlapping a little against her full lip.

Margaret shivered. She-wolf seemed an apt nickname for the tough Frenchwoman.

She pushed her way out into the coolness of the corridor again. She was faint with the heat and wanted only to be alone to think clearly about the idea Jasper had put into her mind. Tomorrow she would leave the Court and make her way to her estates at Sampford Peverell, where Henry Stafford waited for her, along with Elizabeth and young Charles Somerset.

She felt tears come into her eyes. If only time could be reversed so that once more she could live in happiness at Pembroke Castle with those she loved around her. She made a quick prayer to the saints to guard her son from all the forces of evil that had gathered over his young head.

The triumph of King Henry the Sixth was short-lived. Edward gathered together a great army and together with his brothers George of

Clarence and Richard of Gloucester, defeated the Queen at Tewksbury.

Henry Stafford had ridden out to learn how the battle was progressing and Margaret paced the chamber, uttering little prayers, watching the roadway anxiously for a sign that her husband was returning.

"You will wear yourself to a thread," Elizabeth admonished. "What good does it do the cause to worry yourself into a decline?"

"I just cannot sit still when I do not know what is happening," Margaret said, and turned over the pages of her book of gospels seeking comfort from the well-loved lines.

"Well, you need contain yourself no longer," Elizabeth said triumphantly. "I can see my Lord Stafford coming across the lower field."

Margaret was almost faint with apprehension and when Henry Stafford made his way unsteadily towards her, she clasped her hands together for fear of crying out loud. He sank into a chair and Elizabeth hurriedly brought him a cup of wine, helping him to hold it to his lips, his hands were shaking so badly.

His eyes were dull as they looked at Margaret. "Our cause is finished, killed on the battlefield of Tewksbury." He tried to steady himself and Margaret fell on her knees, holding both his hands in hers. "The young Prince of Wales was cruelly slain, right before his mother's eyes. The Queen was mad with grief and it took four of Edmund's men to hold her." He paused for a moment to draw his breath. "I'm sorry to have to tell you, Margaret, but both of your cousins were killed. Edmund, Duke of Somerset, was executed after the battle, and his younger brother John died on the field."

Margaret drew a sharp breath. "All the Somersets are gone," she said, "their blood spilled for England. All except young Charles who was born out of wedlock." She walked over the chamber and stared out at the darkening sky, her eyes moist with tears. "Edward is rid of his enemies now, except for the poor mad King, and I don't expect that any mercy will be shown to him." She spun round quickly and looked beseechingly at Henry. "My son must be taken to France. I will write a letter to Jasper Tudor. They must both leave before Edward thinks of capturing them."

Henry coughed a little. "I will go just as soon as I've had some rest. Don't worry, Margaret, your son will be safe, I promise you.

Margaret rested her head against his sleeve. "You must not ride out again. Send a messenger, someone you can trust. I can see that you are utterly exhausted."

He lifted his hand to her hair. "It is a tiredness of the spirit more than of the body, Margaret. I will send a message; no doubt a younger, stronger man would ride more swiftly."

She helped him up. "Come to your chamber, Henry. You must rest. Elizabeth will bring you a potion to induce sleep and in the morning you will feel much better."

She left him propped against his pillows so that he could breathe more easily and there was a worried frown on her face as she faced Elizabeth.

"He is very ill. I can see it in his face, and in his hands." She walked nervously about the chamber. "What can I do, Elizabeth?"

"Nothing tonight except to rest and see how my Lord Stafford feels in the morning." Elizabeth spoke firmly, though her eyes avoided Margaret's glance.

"I feel it inside my very being that he is not strong. There is surely something I can do to help him."

Elizabeth took her arm. "You go and try to sleep. I will sit with him myself and if he should wake, I will come for you immediately."

Margaret sighed. "Very well. Perhaps I am making a fuss about nothing. We will see what the morning shall bring."

Elizabeth shuddered, her eyes turned away from Margaret so that she should not see the feeling of dread in them. Henry Stafford was ill of the lung fever, though he did not realise it himself and Elizabeth very much doubted that he would live to see another morning.

Night had closed in around the thick mansion walls and in the silence, Margaret's gown whispering along the corridors sounded unnaturally loud. She had no idea what had disturbed her, but she slipped immediately from the sheets and made her way to Henry's chamber.

At the door, Elizabeth, her face white, in the light from the tapers, stood aside for Margaret to enter, and together they walked towards the bed.

"He didn't wake at all," Elizabeth whispered. "He just slipped away quietly in his sleep."

Margaret stood in silence looking down at the man who had been her husband, who had cared for her and comforted her when she was troubled.

"I wasn't even with him," she said brokenly. "I would have prayed with him and held his hand. I might have brought him some comfort."

Elizabeth shook her head. "He didn't wake, Margaret. He would have been unaware of your presence, so don't reproach yourself."

"I will have a priest say perpetual Mass for him at the College of Plessy," she said bleakly. "It is all I can do for him now."

She held herself erect as she left the chamber, and tears slipped unnoticed down her cheeks.

"If only I could have given him more love," she said softly. "Perhaps I could have made him a happier man."

"Nonsense," Elizabeth said bluntly. "He loved you so much that you were all he ever wanted from life. You were good and obedient to him. What more could any man ask?"

Margaret sat in a chair, her hand laying across the book of gospels. "I hope you are right, Elizabeth. I have loved my son so well since my dear

Edmund died that there has been little room for anyone else."

"You have loved little Charles Somerset. He is a fine boy. A credit to your care and teaching."

Margaret nodded her head in agreement. "You speak the truth, Elizabeth, but there is always something selfish in my loving. I just cannot help it."

"You are upset. It is natural that you should reproach yourself. It happens to all who have lost a loved one. Believe me, Henry Stafford was a lucky man, and he knew it, even if you didn't."

Margaret leaned her head wearily on her arms. "I would like to be left alone for a time, if you don't mind," she whispered and as Elizabeth left the room, Margaret knew that the tears falling on to her hands were more for herself than for poor Henry Stafford who lay dead and silent in the next chamber.

Margaret sat upright in her chair, listening almost in a daze to the droning voice of the cleric reading out a list of Henry's behests.

"To Henry, Earl of Richmond, I bequeath a trappar of four new horse harnesses of velvet, and to my brother John, Earl of Wiltshire, my favourite bay courser. The residue of my estates are to be given to my beloved wife Margaret, Countess of Richmond, to do with what she pleases."

When the interminable reading of the will was over, Margaret retired to her chamber and rested her head wearily against the lavender-scented pillow. It was true that she had not loved Henry in the wild sweet way she had loved Edmund, but she had come to have a respect for him and a high regard for his integrity, and life without his steadying hand to hold her was going to be very bleak and lonely.

Elizabeth, in the best of intentions, had suggested that she might marry again in time, but Margaret could not bring herself to even consider such a prospect. Two men had died and left her alone and her son had been continually taken from her side. It seemed she was meant to live a solitary life.

Perhaps she would retire to an Abbey once young Charles was old enough to do without her. It seemed an ideal life; no cares or tribulations from the world outside, just prayer and meditation and endless peace of mind.

She closed her eyes and the steady drone of voices in the outer chamber soothed her, until at last she fell into a sound, dreamless sleep.

CHAPTER SIXTEEN

Elizabeth moved slowly through the garden, bright with spring flowers. At her side was young Charles of Somerset. His thin form had begun to fill out, his shoulders broadened, giving him a manly appearance in spite of his tender years.

"Why is the Lady Margaret crying?" he asked abruptly.

Elizabeth looked at him in surprise. "There's not much misses your eyes my lad," she smiled at him reassuringly. "There's nothing that you need concern yourself with."

He stopped walking. "I heard the servant talking about some ladies who have died. They were sorry for Margaret, because it is not very long ago that Uncle Henry was laid to rest."

Elizabeth clucked her tongue. "You had no business listening to gossip, but since you've asked I supposed I'd better tell you." She drew him to the low wall that bordered the garden, and sat down awkwardly. "I'm growing so stout these days I can't bear to stand still for too long." She patted the wall. "Come, sit next to me. It's lovely here in the sun." She waited until he was seated. "Now, the ladies you talked about are the Duchess of Somerset, Margaret's mother, and the Duchess of Buckingham."

"Uncle Henry's mother?" Charles asked in

surprise. "I didn't know his mother was still alive even?"

Elizabeth smiled. "I know what you mean. She was very old, of course, but Margaret is naturally upset at the double loss."

Charles, his curiosity satisfied, rose impatiently from the wall. "I'll race you back, Elizabeth," he said playfully, and set out with long strides across the garden.

Elizabeth watched him a little sadly. He was already being called the Somerset bastard in Court circles, and was fast coming to an age when such names would cause him hurt. All the same, he had a good protector in Margaret. She would ensure that he was treated with respect — at least in her presence.

She followed Charles more slowly, and as she rounded a curve in the garden, she saw that Charles had collided with Margaret, who had taken him in her arms to prevent them both from falling.

"Where does the boy get his energy?" she smiled ruefully at Elizabeth, straightening her headdress. "Go along to your studies, Charles. I would like to speak to Elizabeth for a moment in private."

He made them both a stiff bow and set off at a run once more, his hair flying behind him.

"He is a charming boy," Elizabeth said fondly. "He will make someone a good husband, one day."

Margaret smiled. "He is every inch a

Somerset," she said sadly. "What a pity he wasn't born in wedlock. He would have a great future before him."

Elizabeth threw back her head and laughed. "Bless you, Margaret, that one would charm the birds from the trees. He will always land on his feet, believe me."

"Perhaps you are right." Margaret walked on in silence for a moment and Elizabeth could see she had something on her mind.

"Try not to brood on the sadness of the past months," Elizabeth said. "It is spring again. The flowers are growing and the sun shines. You should look to the future."

"That is just what I am doing," Margaret said, and smiled a little sadly. "I am having a visitor this evening."

Elizabeth looked at her in surprise. "A visitor? Well, why all the secrecy? This is the first I have heard of it?"

"Do I have to ask your permission to have a gentleman pay me court?" Margaret raised her eyebrows and regarded Elizabeth steadily.

"Come on," Elizabeth said impatiently, "tell me who it is. Don't keep me in suspense any longer."

"Thomas Stanley. There, now you know." Margaret stopped underneath the blossoming apple tree. "I can't say what will come of the meeting; perhaps nothing at all, but as you say, I must look to the future, mine and that of my son."

Elizabeth stared at her in amazement. "But Margaret, Lord Stanley has so many children. You don't know what you're taking on!"

"I do know." Margaret counted on her fingers. "There are the twins, John and George; then Richard, Edward, James, Thomas and William. And the girls, Anne, Alice, Catherine and Agnes. Eleven of them in all! He must have been running out of names!"

Elizabeth lifted her hands in the air. "Saints preserve us! They won't all come to live here, will they?"

She couldn't see what Margaret would gain from such a match. It certainly wouldn't be peace and quiet.

Margaret looked directly at her. "He is called the wily fox, and not for nothing! He changed his allegiance from Henry to King Edward in a twinkling of an eye. He now holds the position of the King's privy councillor." She sank down wearily on to the soft grass, her gown billowing around her, like a purple flower. "He can offer me his protection in exchange for some of my estates, and those I can well afford to do without." She smoothed back a strand of hair that hung over her forehead. "Who knows, he may be persuaded to change his coat again when the time comes."

"I don't know what nonsense this is you are talking, but I don't think you can be in your right senses to even think of such a thing."

Margaret lifted her face to the bright bowl of the sky and the sun was like a Benediction bathing her in brightness and warmth.

"The saints will watch over me and over my son. As for Lord Stanley, I am quite able to take care of him," she said with a secret smile.

"Please, my lord, help yourself to a little more meat." Margaret leaned across the table, smiling warmly at Thomas Stanley. "The peacock is delicious; and the fish has been cooked in a wine brought especially from France."

"Both dishes look so appetising, I think I shall sample a little of each." He speared some food on the blade of his knife and smiled amiably at Margaret. "I think we can dispense with the formalities now. Please do me the honour of calling me Thomas."

Margaret inclined her head. "Willingly, if you will call me Margaret."

He took her fingers and kissed them elegantly. "A beautiful name for a beautiful lady."

She hid a smile, knowing full well that his compliments had no substance to them. It came easily to him to flatter any woman he happened to find himself with.

He had brought a few of his younger children with him and it had not escaped Margaret's notice that among their attendants was a beautiful young girl with pink skin and corn-coloured hair who had eyes for no one but Thomas Stanley. Margaret had summed up their relationship very quickly, and was quite pleased by her findings.

When the preliminaries were over, Margaret rose from the table and Thomas followed her into the small chamber. He stood over her, a tall figure of a man, with a square jaw and small eyes that were full of humour.

"Well, Margaret, have you thought about my proposal yet? I am impatient for a reply."

"My answer is yes," Margaret said at once. "But there are certain conditions."

"Naturally, my dear," Thomas said affably, "there always are to any bargain."

He would have put out his arms to embrace her, but she moved away out of reach.

"I would like to be honest with you, Thomas," she said calmly. "My reasons for wanting a husband are many-fold, but affection or desire are not numbered among them."

He looked at her with surprise.

"I do not wish for more children," Margaret said quickly, "and in any event I am too old to risk a confinement." She smiled at him. "Fortunately you are adequately endowed with heirs. The Lady Eleanor was a good wife in that respect, for which fact I feel sure you are most grateful."

"Just a minute, Margaret," he said suddenly. "Am I to understand that you do not wish the marriage to be consummated?"

"I'm glad you understand, my lord," she said sweetly. "Please accept these gifts from me as a mark of my good faith."

He took the documents from her hand, still

looking a little bewildered.

"Read them, Thomas," she said. "I have made over to you for life, the manors of Bedehampton, Woking, Sutton, Tydhurst, the hundreds of Lyghtfeld, oh! and several others. But please read for yourself."

"My dear Margaret, you are most generous; the list is endless."

She smiled. "Not quite, but perhaps the sum of eight hundred marks every year will prove useful to you."

He held out his hand, and after a moment's hesitation, she took it.

"I will arrange a suitable settlement for you, my dear. I'm sure we will have a good arrangement between us." He coughed delicately. "I would like to keep one or two of my favourite attendants near me. I trust you would have no objections?" He smiled suavely, and Margaret smiled in spite of herself.

"Your own comforts shall remain your concern, Thomas. I shall not interfere. You may be sure of that."

He nodded, well pleased. "Now that our business is concluded to our mutual satisfaction, it might be a good idea to show our happy smiling faces to the public." He winked and placed his arm around her shoulders.

She allowed the embrace, smiling at him respectfully. Thomas was indeed a wily fox, and if their marriage was to be one of convenience, he had decided that no one but themselves should be allowed to know it.

Derby House overlooked Saint Benet's hill, and Margaret was delighted with the tall stately rooms and the gracious gardens of her new London home.

"I think you will be happy here," Thomas smiled. "I have always loved this house, and the children would be upset if I were to suggest making a move."

Margaret seated herself near the window. "It is wonderful to hear the sound of children laughing once more," she said a little wistfully, and Thomas moved immediately to her side.

"That is a problem I can be relied upon to solve!" He smiled mischievously at her, and she felt her colour rise.

"I have told you my views on that score," she said firmly. "You confine yourself to your already existing family. I should think there are enough of them to satisfy the most exacting of men!"

She could not suppress the smile that curved her lips and Thomas threw back his head and laughed.

"I think we are both missing out by your sternness, Margaret, but we made a bargain and I won't be the one to break it." He seated himself beside her and took her hand, his expression suddenly serious. "Indeed, fortune is on your side. I am to be sent to Scotland to aid the Duke of Gloucester at Berwick. I know I can trust you to be kind to my children while I am away."

"You can indeed, Thomas. They will brighten my days, and as you can see, Charles has already acquainted himself with some of your sons."

Across the sunlit garden, she heard his young voice raised in excitement.

"Let us go to the butts, I declare I can outshoot any of you. I'll put a mark on it."

The boys streaked across the green, and Margaret smiled proudly.

"I imagine he means what he says. He is fiercely proud of his skill."

"You are kind to the boy," Thomas said thoughtfully. "I suppose he makes up a little for the absence of your son."

"Nothing could do that, but I love Charles very much indeed. I mean to see that in spite of the stigma of his birth, he has every possible advantage."

Thomas got to his feet. "It may be that I can be of some small help in that direction. At any rate, I will drop a word in all the right places."

"Thank you, Thomas. My regard for you becomes stronger every day. It seems I have been more than fortunate in my choice of a husband."

He patted her arm. "I may convince you to fall in love with me yet." He moved to the door. "I will be leaving London some time in the next few days, but I will try to return before too long. After all, we are still newlyweds!"

Margaret leaned back in her chair after he had

gone. The sun was warm on her face and hands, and the shouts of the children in the garden sounded pleasant on the warm air.

She took up the primer that Henry Stafford's mother, the Duchess of Buckingham, had left her, handling it lovingly. It was covered in purple velvet with clasps of silver gilt and it was heavy against her knees.

Unexpectedly, tears came to Margaret's eyes. She thought of Henry, gentle and kind. She had been happy with him in spite of everything, and missed him sorely now that he was gone.

Carefully, she opened the book. In its pages she would find some comfort and help. Reading had always been one of her greatest joys, and now she needed an occupation that would take her mind off the difficulties her new situation would inevitably bring.

"The King is on his death bed!" Thomas Stanley stood at the door of Margaret's chamber, his clothes dusty and travel-stained and his face grey with fatigue.

In an instant Margaret was at his side, leading him to a chair.

"Elizabeth, have someone bring wine for my Lord Stanley. And some broth with plenty of meat." Icy fingers of fear were making her hands shake. "But the King is still in the prime of his life. What could have brought him to this?"

Thomas shrugged broad shoulders. "Some are saying he caught a lung fever by riding out at night to his latest mistress. No one seems very charitable now that the King lies so near to death."

"He was so kind to me," Margaret whispered. "Even though he was a Yorkist King and could have taken everything from me if he had so wished."

"Yes, he was a good King, though the people won't realise it until he is gone. It is always the way."

"What will happen now?" Margaret asked through stiff lips, her hand clutching the cross that hung from her waist.

"Edward's young son will be King in truth, but you know the old saying: 'Woe to thee oh! land when thy king is a child.' It is my belief that if the King dies, his brother, Richard of Gloucester, will take the crown." He took the cup that Elizabeth held towards him, and thankfully drank deep. "He has no love for you, Margaret, or for me if it comes to that! So unless I can do something about it, our future doesn't look too bright."

Margaret sat down, her legs were trembling so much they would not support her. "Do you think it could be a lie? Maybe the King is just down with a slight chill after all."

Thomas shook his head. "I heard it from Mistress Shore herself. She was weeping and almost faint with distress because the Queen will not allow her at the King's side now when he needs her most."

"Poor girl. What will become of her?" Margaret pitied Jane Shore with all her heart. Queen Elizabeth was capable of turning her away without a rag to her back.

"I believe my old friend Lord Hastings intends to take her under his protection. She will be all right, don't fret yourself about her."

Margaret walked across the room and stood before the window. "A moment before you came in, I didn't have a care in the world." She stared out into the softness of the day. "And now my thoughts fly about like pollen on the breeze."

Thomas moved towards her, awkwardly putting his arm around her shoulders. "Trust me," he said slowly. "They don't call me the wily fox for nothing."

The bells tolled dismally across the silent streets of London. King Edward the Fourth was dead, and his people mourned him. Margaret sat alone in her chamber, the summer rain outside the window reflecting her feelings.

"I've brought you a soothing balm, Margaret," Elizabeth said, and carried an overflowing cup, handing it carefully to Margaret. "It will ease the ache that plagues you."

Margaret grimaced at the bitterness of the drink. "Nothing could do that except the release of Lord Stanley from prison."

"He is such a brave man." Elizabeth's voice was tinged with envy. She was more than half in love with Thomas Stanley herself.

"He stood by his friend, Lord Hastings, who took on Jane Shore when the King died."

"Yes," Margaret said wryly. "He fought for Hastings but earned himself a crack on the head with a halbert from one of Richard's men."

"What will happen now, I wonder?" Elizabeth settled herself beside Margaret, waiting hopefully for an answer to her question.

"It very much looks as if Richard means to be King. He has put young Edward and his brother in the tower; poor little boys, my heart aches for them." Margaret's brow was furrowed as she thought of her own son far away in exile across the sea. Perhaps even he was better off than the two young princes.

"Will we be in danger if Richard does become King?" Elizabeth's voice shook a little.

"Oh, no, not actual danger, though no doubt I will be attainted and deprived of my estates." She looked troubled. "I would not mind for myself, but my son will have a difficult time of it without my money to secure his position in France."

"No doubt that hook-backed Richard of Gloucester believes you are too considerate of the Earl of Richmond," Elizabeth said drily. "He fears King Henry's words might yet come true, that your son will unite the red rose and the white, and bring peace to England."

Margaret leaned back wearily in her chair. "I think your potion is beginning to work. I feel pleasantly drowsy."

"Try to sleep then. I will help you to your bed," Elizabeth smiled. "Sleep is the best remedy for all ills, I always say."

Margaret thankfully climbed between the covers and closed her eyes with the strangest feeling that everything was slipping away from between her fingers.

"Well, my sweet Margaret, are you happy to see me returned from prison?" Thomas strode into the room, his face wreathed in smiles, and Margaret struggled to sit up in bed.

"Thomas, how wonderful. But what has happened?" She held out her hand and he took it warmly.

"Richard has decided I am more use to him alive than dead! I am to go to London. Indeed we are both to go and attend him at his coronation!" He kissed her cheek. "Did I not tell you I would sort everything out?"

"I can't believe it. He surely doesn't want me at his coronation!" Margaret said in disbelief.

"Wait until you see the present he has made you!" Thomas waved his hand to the servant to bring in the gifts and Margaret pushed aside the covers excitedly.

"Oh, just look at that dress. There must be a full ten yards of scarlet velvet here in the skirt alone," Elizabeth said, holding the gown up for Margaret to see it better. "Just look at the cloth of gold! Isn't it gorgeous?"

Margaret was suddenly reminded of the ruby

and gold collar presented to her by the Duke of Suffolk, and the thought was like a nasty taste in her mouth.

"Why does Richard of Gloucester send me such a gown?" she asked, looking up at Thomas in bewilderment. "And there in the chest are more gifts. I don't understand."

"You, my dear wife, are to bear the Queen's train." His eyes shone with triumph. "You are to take precedence before all other countesses, and even before the Duchess of Suffolk and Norfolk. You are the most honoured lady in the whole of England." He took her hand, kissing her fingers gently, his gaze meeting hers. "It seems that the reign of Richard the Third is going to be a profitable one for us."

CHAPTER SEVENTEEN

The mellow sun slanted in through the tall windows of Derby House and Margaret, stitching a tracery of delicate leaves into her tapestry work, enjoyed the warmth of the autumn day.

The door opened and Margaret saw with surprise that Thomas was leading a young, golden-haired girl towards her.

"My dear," he said, his eyes alight, "may I present Princess Elizabeth of York, daughter of King Edward."

There was a sudden hush in the chamber as the company waited for Margaret's response. Recovering quickly from her surprise, she drooped into a curtsey and immediately, like roses bending in a gale, the other ladies followed her lead.

"The Princess will be lodging here with us for a time," Thomas said easily. "She has come straight from the sanctuary of Westminster."

Elizabeth of York smiled warmly. "And most happy to be away from there. You are so kind to have me, Lady Margaret."

Margaret inclined her head. "Perhaps you would like to rest? Come, I will show you to our best chamber. I only hope you will be comfortable here."

Elizabeth laughed good-naturedly. "I'm delighted to be in a house that does not ring with the sound of chanting day and night." She glanced at Margaret quickly from under pale lashes. "I don't mean to be irreverent, but the sound of prayers can become monotonous after a time."

Margaret smiled. "I'm sure Westminster must have seemed dull to you after the gaiety of the Court." She paused a moment. "How is your mother, the Dowager-Queen? I trust she is well and in good spirits?"

Elizabeth's expressive face drooped into lines of sadness, and she shrugged her slim shoulders.

"She worries about my young brothers. Poor Edward and little Richard must be missing her sorely."

Margaret warmed to her. She was such an open-hearted girl, obviously capable of great love. Unbidden, the thought entered her mind that the Princess Elizabeth would make an admirable wife for her son, the Earl of Richmond.

For a moment she was back at the Court of the poor mad King Henry the Sixth. He had called the Earl of Richmond England's hope, and declared that he would unite the red rose and the white. Was it possible that somewhere in his disturbed mind he had foreseen the future?

She shuddered a little and brought her attention back to the present.

"Here, my Lady Elizabeth, I hope the chamber will be comfortable."

"It is so warm after the coldness of the abbey.

It is no wonder that monks must wear stout robes. It is to prevent them catching the lung fever!"

Margaret smiled. "If there is anything you need, you have only to ask. I will leave you to rest now."

She closed the door gently, and made her way back to where Thomas was waiting for her.

He took her arm and drew her to one side. "The Duke of Buckingham wishes to talk with you," he said quietly. "He will be on the road between Worcester and Bridgnorth two days from now at about noon. I believe he has a plan he wishes to put to you." He stared down at her warningly. "You must understand that I will disown any knowledge of this if it should come to King Richard's ears."

Margaret clasped his hand, hope building inside her. "It is about my son, is it not?"

He shook his head sagely. "All I know is that you intend to make a visit of devotion to Our Lady of Worcester."

Margaret nodded her understanding, her eyes bright. "It may well be the wish of Our Lady and all the saints that my son return from France," she said quietly and Thomas smiled drily.

"Be sure your prayers are made in discreet tones, that's all I ask," he cautioned.

"I will be very discreet," she said happily. "Wasn't I the soul of discretion at the coronation? Did I not do you justice?"

Thomas kissed her cheek. "I was very proud of

you, Margaret. You were the most beautiful woman there."

She slipped her hand through his arm. "I'm very glad I married you, Thomas Stanley," she said, and her eyes were shining.

"I am delighted to meet you in this way, my lady." The young Duke of Buckingham dismounted from his horse and bent over her hand.

"It is a wonderful coincidence, is it not?" Margaret could not keep the twinkle from her eye. "My word, you grow more like Henry Stafford every day. He will never be dead while you are alive."

Buckingham inclined his head. "You do me honour, my lady. I always did admire Uncle Henry. After all, he had the good taste to make you his wife."

Margaret glanced round at her retinue. "I think I will rest in the shade for a moment. Perhaps, Buckingham, you will be so kind as to accompany me?"

As soon as they were out of earshot, Margaret put her hand on the young Duke's arm.

"What was it you wished to speak to me about? Is it something to do with the Earl of Richmond?"

Buckingham nodded. "Some of us feel that Richard is not the rightful King," he said gruffly. "We feel that Lancaster has the greater claim."

Margaret forced herself to nod and smile pleasantly as if they were discussing nothing more important than the weather.

"I believe you would consider the Princess Elizabeth as wife to your son?" Buckingham spoke rapidly. "If this could be achieved, the Earl would have greater claim to the throne."

"I am prepared to help in any way I can," Margaret smiled up at him. "I have money and you will need a great deal if the plan is to work properly."

"Good, then we will arrange for the Earl to land on the coast of Britain as soon as possible. Have you anyone you can trust to help us, my lady?"

"There is Reginald Bray, Steward of my household. He has been with me for many years. And there is my physician, Lewis. He is a Welshman and would die for the Earl, if necessary."

Buckingham nodded, well pleased. "Your physician can carry messages to the Dowager-Queen in sanctuary without being suspected. We must ask if she is in favour of her daughter marrying the Earl of Richmond." He smiled drily. "I don't expect her to refuse her consent. She is heartily sick of hiding away from Richard, and will agree to any plan that shakes him from the throne." He bowed to her once more. "I will take my leave of you now, Lady Margaret, but I will be in communication with you before long, never fear."

Margaret stood and watched him ride away, and there were tears of gratitude in her eyes.

"May I sit and talk with you for a little while, Lady Margaret?" Princess Elizabeth stood diffidently at the door of Margaret's chamber, her blue eyes as appealing as those of a helpless puppy.

"My dear Lady Elizabeth. I am always at your disposal."

Elizabeth settled herself quietly at Margaret's side, her tapering fingers resting lightly on the velvet cover of the primer Margaret was reading.

"I am not very clever, unfortunately." Elizabeth sounded wistful, and Margaret smiled warmly at her.

"You are young and beautiful, my lady," she said quickly, "and you have a quality of innocence which is very unusual in these troubled days."

Elizabeth held herself in unconscious dignity, her slender neck straight and her head high.

"You are so kind to me, Lady Margaret. I hope one day I may be able to repay you in some measure."

"Don't think any more of it. You are a joy to be with." Margaret leaned forward suddenly. "My lady, do you know that your mother the Queen and I are making plans for your future?" She paused and looked around cautiously. "At the moment they must be kept a secret."

Elizabeth regarded her with trusting blue eyes. "I'm sure any plans that you care to make must be for the good. I will leave myself in your hands." She smiled a little impishly, and a sparkle came into her eyes. "I believe your plan includes your son, and if he is anything like you in character, he must be a very good man."

Margaret put a warning finger to her lips. "Be careful, my dear, I would not like it if you placed yourself in any danger."

Elizabeth was dignified once more. "I have been in danger since my father died. It is not a new companion, but for your sake, I will speak no more about what you have in mind."

Margaret smiled, her liking for the young princess was strengthened with every day they spent together.

"Never mind, Elizabeth. It may soon be that you will never have to think about danger again."

"Lady Margaret, may I speak to you in private?" Lewis bent over her hand, his dark eyes looking directly into hers.

She led him into an inner chamber, her heart beating so quickly that she could hardly breathe.

"In a moment, I will be needing your services!" She smiled and beckoned for him to come and sit at her side.

"The Dowager-Queen agrees to the plan," he said immediately. "She is tired of sanctuary and fears for the lives of the young princes who are still incarcerated in the Tower." He paused, mopping his round face with his kerchief. "It is my belief that she sees the Earl, your son, as no more than regent until Prince Edward is older."

Margaret shook her head. "Does not the Queen realise that there is no chance of her son becoming King while there is evidence that she is not legally married to Edward? Richard himself has taken the crown using the very fact that he regards the boy as illegitimate to consolidate his claim."

Lewis frowned anxiously. "She does not realise how tenuous her own position is. She believes that soon she will come from sanctuary and take once more her place as Queen."

Margaret sighed. "I cannot help but feel sorry for her. Perhaps if the late King had named her as regent, all might have gone well for her, in spite of Richard."

Lewis rose to his feet. "Has the Earl been informed of what is taking place, my lady?" he said, rubbing his plump hands together and Margaret smiled.

"Yes. Hugh Conway has gone to Brittany with a large sum of money for my son. Hugh is a trustworthy friend and I rely on him entirely."

Lewis nodded his greying head. "Quite so, my lady, and may I say I hope with all my heart that fortune smiles on you and the Earl of Richmond."

After her physician had taken his leaves, Margaret went in search of the young princess.

"Lady Elizabeth," she said cordially. "Your mother has agreed to the union. Now all we have to do is wait until my son lands on

England's shores once more."

Elizabeth looked at her quickly. "I am happy for you, my lady, and yet I cannot help feeling sorry for my Uncle Richard. He has always been kind to me."

"Quite right, Elizabeth, you should retain old loyalties. But Richard won't be harmed if he will only accept the situation sensibly." She glanced shrewdly at Elizabeth. "After all, he was never meant to be King, was he?"

"No, of course he wasn't." Tears came to Elizabeth's blue eyes. "If only father had not died so suddenly. None of us were prepared, and my brothers are so young."

"Everything will be all right, if only you will have a little patience, my lady. At least you know that you have your mother's approval in this matter."

Elizabeth sank down into a chair. "Perhaps you will show me those new stitches, Lady Margaret," she said quickly. "I feel I must not think about the future too much, just in case anything goes wrong."

A sudden shadow seemed to settle around Margaret. She quickly made the sign of the cross.

"Don't speak of things going wrong, my lady. We must be hopeful and think of all the good things that are before us."

She brought her tapestry to Elizabeth's side and tried to concentrate on the tiny flowers she was working, but at the back of her mind echoed a small voice that persisted in saying over and over again that nothing must go wrong. At last she rose to her feet.

"Excuse me, my lady," she said quickly, "I must go outside into the fresh air."

But even in the sunshine, a gloom seemed to hang like a mist around her head.

CHAPTER EIGHTEEN

"Something has gone wrong." Margaret paced the room in great agitation, clasping her trembling hands before her in an unconscious gesture of supplication. "If all was well, I would have had news of my son's landing long ago. I can barely endure this waiting."

Elizabeth of York rose from her chair, her young face troubled. "Please do not distress yourself, Lady Margaret. There is always some delay in these matters. The time seems longer to those who wait." She leaned near the sill, her clear skin and bright hair accentuated by the pale sunlight. "You know what they say. No news is good news."

Margaret shook her head. "Not this time. I feel in my bones that something has gone wrong."

She covered her face with her hands, sending up a prayer to the saints that Henry, Earl of Richmond, should be spared Richard's anger if the plot to remove him from the throne had misfired.

"Lady Margaret, someone is riding this way!"

Elizabeth forgot her royal dignity and scrambled on to a chest beneath the window in order to have a better view of the man riding his horse at full gallop across the green.

"It is Reginald Bray. I must hurry to meet him!"

Margaret's gown billowed around her as she took the stairs quickly, her heart pounding fiercely within her.

"My lady." Reginald Bray flung himself from the saddle and knelt at her feet and there were tears on his weather-beaten face.

Margaret's heart turned over in fear. "Tell me at once. Is my son all right?"

"It is all over, my lady." He could not bring himself to look at her. "Heavy rains flooded the Severn, and my Lord Buckingham and his men were unable to ford it."

"But what of the Earl of Richmond?" Margaret asked in anguish.

Reginald shook his head. "I saw nothing of him whatsoever, my lady. It may be that he was warned in time and set sail back to France."

Margaret could scarcely breathe. "And it could be that he lies dead on the shores of England," she said bitterly.

Elizabeth came and took her arm, and with Elizabeth of York supporting Margaret on the other side, together they took her back to the chamber.

Elizabeth hurriedly brought some wine, handing the cups round with fingers that trembled.

Margaret's colour returned somewhat after she had rested for a moment.

"Tell me everything you know, Reginald," she said in a whisper. "Leave nothing out."

He sat opposite her, awkwardly aware of his

mud-stained appearance.

"When the river flooded, my lady, Buckingham was prevented from joining forces with the Courtenays." His tone was bitter. "When it was known that Buckingham was not with us, the Marquis of Dorset and Lord Welles had no choice but to flee the country. I believe they made for Brittany."

"Thank God that at least my brother, Lord Welles, is safe," Margaret said softly. "And what happened to Buckingham?"

"He was basely betrayed by one of his own men." Reginald's face clouded with anger. "When Richard caught up with him at Salisbury, the Duke of Buckingham was immediately executed."

Margaret looked down at her trembling hands with eyes blurred by tears. "He must be safe. The Earl of Richmond must be allowed to try once more to deliver England from the wickedness of Richard the Third."

With an effort, she rose to her feet and made a small curtsey to Elizabeth of York.

"If you will all excuse me, I will retire to my room. I need to be alone for a time, to think and pray."

With shoulders straight, Margaret walked across the long chamber and from her appearance no one would have guessed that her heart was breaking into a hundred pieces.

Thomas stood before the roaring logs, a worried frown on his broad face.

"I'm sorry, Margaret, but the King has ordered me to keep you away from Court. You are to be confined to these chambers, and all of your companions must be sent away lest you bribe someone to carry messages to your son."

Margaret looked down at her hands. In spite of her husband's words there was a look of serenity on her face.

"Very well, Thomas, it shall be as you say. I thank the saints every day for keeping Henry safe, and when the time is right he will try to make for England once more, whether I communicate with him or not."

Thomas knelt before her and took her hands in his.

"You know I would do anything for you. I was hard put to keep you from being charged with treason," he smiled a little ruefully. "I talked so well that I amazed myself as well as King Richard."

"I realise how wonderful you have been to me thoughout this time of worry, and I know how difficult it must have been for you to face the King concerning my actions. It will not be forgotten, I promise you that." She smiled at him warmly. "The time will come when my son, Henry, may be in a position to help you greatly. He will know to whom he owes the greatest debt of gratitude."

Thomas looked uncomfortable. "Margaret, please, you must allow no one to hear you speak that way. It is highly dangerous."

She kissed his cheek gently, her eyes alight. "I have grown very fond of you, Thomas Stanley. Could it be that our marriage has turned out to be more than one of convenience after all?"

He smiled and shook his head. "I will never understand women if I live to be a hundred. They swing from one subject to another so easily, and I am a mere man and completely baffled."

He kissed her fondly, and for a moment, Margaret thought she saw a tear sparkle on his dark lashes. But then he was on his feet.

"I cannot stay here, idling my time away." He sounded gruff. "I must ride back to Court to see if Richard's mood has improved a little during my absence."

He stood near the door for a last look at her; then he made her a quick bow and left her alone.

The days passed quickly, and Richard's mood did not improve. He continued to regard Margaret, Countess of Richmond, as his bitter enemy.

Once more, Thomas Stanley returned home to inform her of the King's latest move against her.

"My dear Margaret, there was nothing I could do." Thomas raised his hands expressively. "The King has called a Parliament which has passed bills of attainer against the Earl of Richmond and yourself."

She looked up at him with tears in her eyes. "So my son will be made a penniless rebel! How could you allow it?"

Thomas sighed deeply. "Have you any idea of the seriousness of your act?" He strode to and fro in agitation. "In Richard's own words, you have conspired and committed high treason against him." He stopped pacing and stood before her. "It is only the King's fear of turning me against him that has saved your life!"

Margaret bowed her head. "I know. I'm sorry, Thomas. I'm afraid I wasn't thinking straight."

"Come, don't be downcast." He smiled at her jovially. "The King still trusts me. He has given me the position of Constable of England in place of Buckingham, and all your estates are transferred to me for life, so you may still regard them as your own."

Margaret looked at him in surprise. "Why is Richard being so generous to you? Surely he suspects that you were involved with me in the plot to put my son on the throne?"

"But I was not involved! Not in the least. You see, my dear, I took the wisest course. They do not call me the wily fox for nothing!"

Margaret smiled in spite of herself. "I know you were not with me in my plan, but you were not against me either."

"That's right," Thomas said drily, "though as the days go by, I begin to be more and more convinced that Henry Richmond would make a better King than Richard the Third."

Margaret's eyed widened. "Do you mean you would help us?" Colour flooded into her face and her breath almost left her.

His face was inscrutable. "I will look into the matter, Margaret. But you must not expect too much." He smiled down at her. "Now I want you to put on your prettiest gown and we will eat here in your chamber. We will drink wine and laugh and forget our troubles just for tonight. How do you feel about that?"

She nodded, catching his mood. "Very well, Thomas. I haven't been very good company lately, but I'll try to make it up to you."

She chose her blue velvet gown trimmed with fur and jewelled at the shoulders and cuffs. The new lady of the bedchamber was deft, and her fingers moved swiftly and surely, braiding Margaret's hair and settling a pearl-stuffed coif on her head.

She stepped out of her chamber feeling much more cheerful than she'd been for days. Thomas was right; it was time she took herself in hand. There was nothing to be gained from moping around the place in a bad humour.

It seemed very quiet in the corridor and Margaret made her way to the great hall, a feeling of apprehension slowing her steps. She pushed open the doors and the chill of emptiness greeted her as she stared along the empty walls. She heard a step behind her and turned to see Thomas, his forehead furrowed into a frown, walking towards her.

"Where has everyone gone?" she said in confusion, hardly able to think straight.

He took her arm and led her back to the chamber. "I said we would eat in your room, didn't I?" he reproved gently. "I didn't want you to know tonight, but the fact is, I've sent everyone away as the King commanded."

"What about my friend, Elizabeth?" Margaret said in consternation. "She has been with me ever since I was a child at Bletsoe. I cannot manage without her."

"You must manage without her, at least for the time being." Thomas led her into the warmth of her own room and settled her into a chair. "They have all gone, including Princess Elizabeth of York. She has returned to her mother in sanctuary. She will at least be safe there."

"What do you mean?" Margaret asked quickly. "Did Richard threaten her?"

"Not exactly," Thomas said. "There was talk that he wished to marry her himself."

"But that's impossible!" Margaret was outraged. "He has a wife already."

"She is ailing and isn't expected to live long. As I said, it is only talk, so far."

Margaret was silent for a moment, then she looked up at Thomas anxiously. "Is young Charles Somerset taken away from me too? And Reginald Bray? And my good physician, Lewis?"

He nodded his head. "It will only be for a short time, Margaret. Once the King's anger dies, he will forget all this and gradually I shall be able to return your loved ones to you."

She fingered her cross. "It was bad enough before, to endure life waiting and hoping for news of my son, but now without my friends around me, I shall be desolate."

"I will do my utmost to bring Elizabeth back to you. I know how much you mean to each other. She cried bitter tears when she was forced to leave."

Margaret blinked quickly. Her own eyes filled with tears, thinking of Elizabeth with her homely, ample proportions, cast away from the home and the people that she loved.

"I have become like a daughter to her," she said softly. "She will pine so badly. I must have her back."

Thomas patted her hand kindly. "I have said I will do my best, my dear." He sat down at the table. "In the meantime, you will have to make do with the servants I have provided. Now let me see you eat a little meat and drink. Some of this sparkling wine will put colour back into your cheeks. And you must keep up your strength, my dear."

To please him, Margaret ate a little, though the food was like dry dust in her mouth. Never in all her life had she felt so desolate, and a cloud of utter hopelessness seemed to hover above her head.

"Elizabeth! Oh, how good it is to see your

happy face again." Margaret, torn between tears and laughter, hugged her friend and then turned to embrace her husband. "Thomas, you are so very good to me. How did you manage to bring Elizabeth home?"

He smiled in mock innocence. "Do you know each other? What a coincidence. This dear lady just happened to be looking for a place to stay and I thought she would make an ideal companion for my wife. If you know each other, then it is no concern of mine."

"Oh, Elizabeth, I've missed you so much," she smiled through her tears. "I have had no one to scold me into resting, and no one to mix up healing potions when I have been chilled. I don't know how I have managed without you."

Thomas smiled good-naturedly over their heads. "Perhaps, my dear wife, you would spare me just one moment of your time," he said wryly, "though I realise that I am interrupting your delirious reunion."

Margaret turned to him contritely. "Thomas, I can't thank you enough, but I think you must know how I feel."

He bent towards her and kissed her cheek lightly. "The happiness in your face is reward enough for me," he said. "But before the both of you run off to compare notes, I would like to speak to you."

Margaret nodded. "You go ahead to my chamber, Elizabeth. I will join you in a moment." Margaret turned to Thomas and led the way to the wide window seat. "What is it, my lord? Not more bad news, I trust?" She regarded him steadily, though her heart was beating rapidly and fear clutched at her with icy fingers.

"There is nothing for you to worry about, my dear," he said quickly. "It is just that I must go away for a time. The King has granted me leave to go up to my estates in Lancashire. I have told him I have business to attend to while I am there." He smiled at Margaret. "It is a fabrication, of course. I just feel I'd be better off away from the Court for the present time."

She looked up at him questioningly. "Are you telling me you have come over to the side of my son?" she asked breathlessly.

Thomas shook his head. "I will say just this, Margaret. I feel there is a great deal of merit in your son's claim to the throne, and Richard has no real right to be King. He virtually stole the crown from young Prince Edward, and you know I have never agreed with having the princes locked away in the Tower." He frowned thoughtfully. "I would feel better about it, if Richard had brought the boys out to make public appearances on occasions, and so would the people. It is being rumoured that the princes are dead — murdered."

"Oh no! Richard could not be so heartless as to have two small children done to death; and the sons of his brother at that." Margaret shuddered, her eyes dark with horror.

"I don't say that Richard would have ordered

such a thing himself, but he is away so often on campaigns. One of his followers might have thought it wiser to put the princes out of the way."

"It does not bear thinking about," Margaret said, and hastily made a sign of the cross. "What must the Dowager-Queen be suffering locked away in Westminster, unable to lift a finger to help her own children?"

"Remember, there is no proof of this, Margaret. It may simply be an evil piece of gossip put about by Richard's enemies. In any event, do not let the servants hear you utter a word of it. They are all in Richard's service, and have been sent here to keep a check on your actions."

Margaret put her hand on his arm and he gently drew her close to him.

"You have become very dear to me, Margaret. There is nothing I wouldn't do to make you happy, but I beg you to be cautious, if not for your own sake, for the sake of your son. Let Richard believe that you have given up any notion of helping the Earl of Richmond to land on the shores of England again."

Margaret smiled up at him from the warm circle of his arms. "I can promise you this, my lord. Henry Richmond will not land on English shores again." She laughed, enjoying his bewilderment.

"Have you really given up all your plans, then?" He looked at her almost with dismay.

She shook her head. "Not at all. But my son

will return through the land that was his father's. He will sail into the tiny harbour of Dale, on the coast of Wales. There are many to follow him from there — supporters of my brother-in-law Jasper Tudor, and his father Owen before him. And this time, my lord, he will be successful. I know it as surely as I breathe."

Thomas stared at her almost fearfully. "You speak with such conviction, Margaret. I cannot help but believe you are right. But where have you received this information? I did not know you were still in touch with your son."

Margaret's eyes gleamed. "There are some things, Thomas, that are best kept secret."

He looked at her in admiration. "For a frail woman, you have a will of steel, Margaret. I'd prefer to be with you than against you."

Margaret smiled softly. "I feel the same way about you, my dear Thomas. It seems to have turned out that we are a pair well matched. The more I think about it, the more I believe it."

His eyes were warm as they met hers, and the kiss he bestowed on her was like the sealing of a promise.

CHAPTER NINETEEN

The pale spring sunshine spilled honey-coloured pools of light on to the floor, and the scent of early flowers gently reminded Margaret of her childhood days at Bletsoe. She sighed softly, and Elizabeth looked up from her sewing.

"Are you troubled about something, Margaret?" she said at once.

Margaret shook her head. "Just thinking of old times, when I was a child at Bletsoe. Do you remember the collar of gold and rubies I was made to wear because the Duke of Suffolk had given it to me? How I hated it."

Elizabeth smiled. "You were such a pretty child; and still your cheeks are as fine-boned and unlined as they were then."

It was true. Margaret had the glow of good health in her skin and her hair was as glossy as a young girl's.

"You pay a pretty compliment, Elizabeth, but I assure you I do not feel young." Margaret went to the window and leaned on the sill. "My son is a grown man now; in his twenty-seventh year. I am in my fortieth year. Time flies so quickly, I can hardly believe it."

"You were so young to be a bride — a mere child." Elizabeth's eyes were moist. "And then to have your husband taken from you so suddenly, and following that, the birth of your son.

There will never be a year like your thirteenth summer."

"It is all a long time ago," Margaret said. "But I still remember Edmund as if it happened yesterday."

Elizabeth put down her needlework. "Shall I bring in some refreshments before we grow too maudlin?" she asked with a glimmer of humour.

"That is a sensible suggestion, Elizabeth," Margaret laughed. "I must be older than I thought to be reminiscing about old times, this way."

Elizabeth went to the door and Margaret heard her speak sharply to Cecile. The girl had been sent to Margaret by King Richard and no doubt she had orders to report anything unusual that might take place.

"Lazy child! She does nothing but sit outside doors listening." Elizabeth's plump face was red with exertion. "I'd be quicker going to the kitchens myself, but I don't see why she shouldn't be made to work."

"It's not her fault if Richard chooses to send her here. I expect she would much rather be back in the gaiety of the Court."

Margaret smiled tolerantly. Just at that moment, Cecile returned with a tray of marchpane, a sullen, angry look on her young face.

"Have you heard the latest gossip about King Richard?"

Elizabeth leaned forward and Margaret's heart skipped a beat.

"It is wise to keep a still tongue in your head, don't you think so?" she said quickly.

But Elizabeth was determined to have her way. "It seems he wishes to marry his niece, Elizabeth of York. I expect the Pope will grant dispensation to the King."

Cecile took a deep breath, her face flooded with colour as she placed the tray before Margaret.

"The King is not himself lately," she said defensively. "He has lost first his son and then his dear wife, and I just don't think you should repeat stupid gossip, Lady Elizabeth."

Cecile finished speaking and stood trembling, waiting to spring to the King's defence again if necessary.

Margaret waved her hand. "Take no notice, Cecile. I think Elizabeth is making sport of you."

Cecile shook her head. "I have heard the rumours too, Countess, and they should be stamped out. Richard would not do such a thing. He has declared the Woodvilles illegitimate, so I hardly think he would marry one of them."

Elizabeth trilled with laughter. "You think that Richard is so holier than thou? Didn't he snatch the throne from his brother's children? And where are those little innocent boys now?"

Cecile clenched her fists. "I have heard that the Princess Elizabeth is being forced to marry Henry, Earl of Richmond, who has been banished from England this many long year!" She stopped and clapped her hand over her lips, re-alising she had gone too far.

Margaret rose to her feet and stood in digni-fied silence for a moment, her face drained of colour. "You may leave us now, Cecile," she said at last, moving across to the warmth of the fire.

"I'm sorry, Margaret." Elizabeth put her arm contritely around Margaret's shoulder. "I shouldn't have tormented the girl. It was all my fault."

"The day will come when everyone will look up to my son." Margaret spoke quietly. "All his life he has been punished for deeds others have committed, but soon, now, England will know that Henry Richmond is a force to be reckoned with."

The long shadows of evening cast strange shapes across the chamber and Margaret stirred, distracted from her prayers by a gentle knocking on the door.

"Please come in," she said quickly, imagining it was Elizabeth coming to remonstrate with her for spending too much time at her devotions.

It was Cecile, her head bent and her eyes avoiding Margaret's gaze.

"It is a bishop, my Lady Margaret. Bishop Morton. He wishes to speak with you."

"I will see him in the other chamber. Are the tapers lit? It is growing dark in here!"

Margaret forced herself to be calm, though her heart was beating so quickly she could scarcely breathe. The Bishop must have brought news of Henry, there was no other reason for his visit.

She moved towards the outer chamber, her hands clasped together as she attempted to appear calm.

"Lady Margaret, how good of you to receive me. I trust you are well?"

Margaret smiled politely, noticing the strong line of the Bishop's face, and his dark piercing eyes.

She dismissed Cecile and waited until the door was closed behind the girl before speaking.

"You have news of my son, my Lord Bishop?" she said hopefully, her voice scarcely obeying her.

He sat down near to her. "The Earl of Richmond is well. He sends his affectionate regard and asks me to tell you that he will return some time in August."

"So soon? Oh, my lord bishop, how I long to see Henry again. Will everything go well this time, do you think?"

He nodded. "I believe so; it is the will of God, Countess. The last attempt was merely a trial run. If you look at it that way, it doesn't seem so bad."

Tears came to Margaret's eyes. "Was he hurt when he attempted to land in England? I have heard nothing except small snippets of gossip."

Bishop Morton shook his head. "Your son forced his way as far as Poole, and when he re-alised there was no army to meet him, he returned to the coast and then to France."

Margaret felt almost light-headed with relief. She sank back into her chair and closed her eyes for a moment, trying to imagine her son as a fully grown man. All she could conjure up in her mind's eye was her husband Edmund, his bright hair shining in the sun.

"This must have been a very trying time for you, my lady."

Margaret became aware that the Bishop was talking to her. Reluctantly she brought her mind back to the present.

"I'm sorry, my lord, you were saying?"

"We have heard how you were attainted and your estates taken from you. No doubt they will be returned to you when your son is King."

He looked about him, aware that here in England the words he spoke were treason.

Margaret went to the door and opened it quietly and there stood Cecile, her eyes wide and her lips trembling.

"I'm sorry, my lady," she murmured. "I did not wish to spy on you."

Margaret drew her inside. "Now please don't start crying. That will do no good at all."

Bishop Morton looked askance at Margaret as she led the weeping girl into the chamber.

"Richard sent her to me," Margaret explained. "He deprived me of my companions and my servants, and placed only his loyal subjects in my household."

"Let her run back to Richard," Morton said

forcefully. "She has heard nothing that would do him the slightest good."

Cecile began to cry out loud and Margaret put her arm around the girl's shaking shoulder.

"Please, Cecile, do not distress yourself. No one is going to hurt you." She handed the girl a kerchief and sat her down near the blazing logs. "You must calm yourself, Cecile. Why are you crying so much?"

"I do not know what to think or feel," the girl gulped noisily. "When I came here to serve you, I imagined that you would be hateful and a true enemy of King Richard. But now, my lady, I don't know what I must do."

Margaret looked at her sympathetically. "You heard what my Lord Bishop was saying?"

The girl nodded. "I know that the Earl of Richmond is going to land on English shores in August; but I do not wish to betray you to the King, my lady, and yet it clearly is my duty."

Morton's eyes glinted. "Tell the King, my dear young lady. You will not be thought any the worse of because of your conflicting loyalties."

Cecile looked up at Margaret, her moist eyes begging for forgiveness. She rose timidly from her chair.

"I'm sorry, Lady Margaret," she said humbly. "I would do anything rather than hurt you, but my first loyalty is towards the King." She started towards the door. "Perhaps you could call off the invasion of England, and then your son would be safe."

Margaret opened her mouth to speak, but the Bishop took Cecile's arm and accompanied her to the door.

"Don't worry your little head over problems that do not concern you, my dear."

Cecile threw a last agonised glance at Margaret, but then the Bishop was closing the door, and she was forced to turn away.

"Why do you allow her to return to the King, my Lord Bishop?" Margaret said slowly. "Is it that you want him to be misinformed about the place my son will land?"

"Of course!" Morton smiled, his dark eyes lighting up in triumph. "The King will guard the English coast, but he will not think of Henry landing on the shores of Wales." He took her fingers and held them to his lips. "Remember, Lady Margaret, when your son reaches the throne of England, he will bring with him peace and prosperity. It is God's will."

Margaret bowed her head, and with eyes closed she prayed that Henry would be kept safe from all his enemies.

Whispers were spreading all over England, turning the blood of good citizens into water as they listened to horrifying tales of the King's wrong-doing.

Margaret sat at home in Derby House stricken to the heart with pity for the Dowager-Queen Elizabeth.

"I don't believe that even Richard could do

away with two innocent young boys." Elizabeth stabbed her tapestry work violently with her needle, venting her anger on the nearest object to hand.

"It is true enough," Margaret said gently, "though I can't believe that Richard did the deed with his own hand. My Lord Stanley believes that one of the King's ministers thought it politic to be rid of the princes. And now it seems that questions are being asked all over the country-side." She sighed. "The only way Richard could clear his name would be to bring young Edward and Richard forth from the Tower, and it seems that he will not, or cannot, do that."

"They are dead then, poor little mites. How I pity the Queen. She must be eating her heart out for her sons." Margaret looked down unseeingly at her tapestry. "Yet Cecile told me that Richard had ordered suits of armour for the boys. I cannot believe he would wish them dead." She shrugged her shoulders. "It may be that we will never know the truth of the mystery, but without a doubt, the boys have disappeared as if from the face of the earth."

"I've heard that their sister, the young Princess Elizabeth, weeps unceasingly for them, and more because her beloved uncle is accused of the double murder."

There was a sudden knocking on the closed door of Margaret's chamber which startled her so much that she dropped her tapestry on to the floor.

Elizabeth rose to her feet, the colour leaving her cheeks as she looked uncertainly at Margaret.

In the silence, the knock was repeated, and Margaret made a visible effort to gather her wits about her.

"Open it, Elizabeth," she said a little shakily, half expecting to see a battalion of the King's guards waiting outside.

"Oh, Lady Margaret, please forgive me for arriving like this!"

Cecile almost stumbled into the room and Margaret helped the distraught girl to a chair.

"What on earth are you playing at?" Elizabeth said quickly. "We all thought you were back at Court with the King."

Cecile drew a deep breath. "I know. I did return to Richard, and I told him, my lady, about the Earl's intention to land in England some time during August." She drew a shuddering breath. "I *had* to tell him. Please believe me, it was my duty."

Margaret nodded. "I understand that, but what brings you here now in such a state?"

"It's about Lord Stanley, Lady Margaret." Cecile loosened her cloak as if unable to breathe. "King Richard does not trust him any longer. He means to demand that Lord Stanley returns to his side or else send his son, Lord Strange, in his place."

Margaret attempted to hide her fear. "But why has the King lost faith in my husband? He has spoken no treason, or committed any act that could be held disloyal to Richard."

"There are rumours that Lord Stanley is inclined to come over to the side of the Earl of Richmond, and the King has repeatedly asked for his return to Court without success." Cecile's words spilled over each other in her anxiety to have them said.

"It was brave of you to come, but are you not placing yourself in danger?" Margaret said quietly.

"I had to come, my lady. Lord Stanley was always kind to me, and I thought I might be able to help in some small way."

Margaret nodded her head. She knew what Cecile was too polite to say, that there had been no conspiracy on Stanley's part. It was only between Margaret and Bishop Morton that the treasonable conversation had taken place.

"Rest here for a little while, and then I will have someone take you back to Court before your absence is noticed."

Margaret spoke kindly, aware that Cecile had taken a great risk in returning to her household.

Elizabeth came close to Margaret. "Can we not warn Lord Stanley about the King's intentions?"

Margaret smiled. "Do you think my husband does not know? He is called the wily fox, remember! He probably knows the King's thoughts before they are uttered."

"What do you think he will do? Will he return

to Richard's Court, do you think?"

Margaret shook her head. "That I cannot answer. My husband is a closed book. No one knows which course he will take. I do know this; he will not endanger the life of his eldest son, and I would not expect or wish him to do that." Margaret felt a thrill of excitement move through her. "It is beginning, Elizabeth. The wheels are set in motion. Soon my son will be here on this very soil. How I've missed him!"

Tears blurred her eyes and she smoothed them away with shaking hands.

"Do not upset yourself, Margaret. That silly child has stirred us all up, and maybe it is all false. She probably didn't understand half of what the King said."

Margaret shook her head. "You underestimate her," she said quietly. "Cecile may be young and sometimes foolish, but she has intelligence of mind far beyond her years, and a conscience that drives her mercilessly." Margaret returned to the girl. "Come, Cecile, drink a little wine. You will feel better soon."

Cecile drew herself up and pulled her cloak around her shoulders once more. "Perhaps I was wrong to come here like this, my lady," she said tiredly. "I don't know where my loyalties lie any longer; but I know I must return to King Richard's Court." She attempted a smile. "May God and all the saints go with you, my lady."

She moved towards the door, pulling her hood over her bright hair, and left the room without once turning back.

"Poor girl!" Elizabeth was moved almost to tears. "I have misjudged her, believing her to be an empty-headed child."

Margaret smiled sadly. "It is easy to misjudge people. In these troubled times it is difficult for anyone to know who is right and who is wrong." She moved slowly across the chamber and stood looking into the bright blaze of the fire. "Sometimes it occurs to me that I might be wrong in wishing my son to be King of England."

She looked so dispirited that Elizabeth put her arm around Margaret's shoulder.

"His destiny was fixed a long time ago, Margaret. Remember the old woman who took us in near London Bridge? She told you even then that your son would wear the crown of England." She smiled reassuringly at Margaret. "King Henry the Sixth himself called the Earl the hope of England. No, you are not wrong, Margaret, your son was meant to be the last of the Lancastrian line. It is the will of God."

"Of course you are right, Elizabeth. I must not lose heart now when the end is so near." She put a hand to her aching head. "It is so easy to become confused and doubtful when people are suffering on every side."

"Keep up your courage, Margaret, it will all turn out as you hope, because it was meant to be."

Margaret smiled. "Your words give me fresh courage, Elizabeth."

She went slowly to her chamber and sank down on the bed, a feeling of utter weariness dulling her senses. She loosened her hair from the tight braids, and it hung loose, still as shining as it had been when she was a girl.

What would her son think of her now? Would she seem very old and changed to his young eyes?

Slowly she lay down, her eyes closing almost against her will. She would sleep for a little while and then she would be fresh to face whatever was to come. Soon now, the long loneliness would be over. Her son would return to take his place at her side. She smiled softly. This time, she knew it in her bones, he would return as a victor!

CHAPTER TWENTY

"Your son has landed on the coast of Wales, Margaret!"

Thomas was still breathless from his ride. Beads of perspiration stood out on his broad forehead, and his cheeks were red from the searing heat of the August day.

Margaret stood still, her eyes closed in prayer. Hot particles of light pierced her lids.

Impatiently, Thomas caught her hands and drew her inside away from the curious stares of his men.

"He has landed at Dale, in Milford Haven, and with the help of the Earl of Oxford, he is raising a great army," he smiled triumphantly. "Soon he will begin to march northwards. My brother, William, is justicular of Wales. He will allow the Earl to proceed unhindered."

"Oh, Thomas, now that the moment is actually here, I feel frightened. What if my son should be wounded, or even killed?"

She clasped his arm and he drew her towards her chair, a reassuring smile on his face.

"Don't you believe he was meant to be King?" he said kindly. "Nothing will happen to him if it is God's will for him to rule England."

Elizabeth hurried to Margaret's side. "What is it? You look so pale. Not bad news, I trust?"

Margaret shook her head. "He is here. My son

has arrived from France. Even now he moves northward. Oh! Elizabeth, how can I bear the waiting?"

"Calm yourself, my lady, nothing will be achieved in a day. It will take weeks for the Earl to gather a large enough army."

Margaret looked at Thomas. He was risking his life by being here, and by speaking of the Earl's presence in Wales. For the first time she realised how much he must care for her.

"Thomas, I am failing in my wifely duties. I have not thought to ask if you are hungry, or thirsty. Please forgive me."

She made to rise from her chair, but Thomas shook his head, smiling warmly at her.

"I have no time to stop, Margaret. And Richard must not know that I have been here."

"I will not allow you to leave until you have at least partaken of a light refreshment. You look hot and dusty and very tired. Please say you will stay for a little while."

He hesitated for a moment, and then began to smile. "Very well. How can I resist when you plead so beautifully?"

Elizabeth turned to the door. "I will instruct the servants, Margaret. Shall they bring the food up to the chamber?"

"Yes," Margaret nodded. "I think that is the best idea. Now I imagine you could do with a little sleep before you set off again, Thomas. Just an hour, so that you can recover your strength."

"All right. You have won me over!"

Margaret rose from her chair and went across to the window. "I wish I could see him before the battle, Thomas. I wonder, is he tall as his father was? Is his hair still as bright and red?" She clasped her hands, her eyes shining with happiness. "This time he *will* succeed, Thomas! I know it, just as surely as the sun is shining."

Thomas smiled. "I believe you, my dear Margaret, I'd be a fool not to, when you look like that."

She rested her hand on his arm. "Thomas, you are so good to me, I don't know what I would have done without you when the King attainted me and ordered my lands to be taken away. If it hadn't been for your cleverness, I would be left with nothing."

There was a clatter of dishes and the servants entered with a tray of cold meat, and a dish of crusty pies.

Elizabeth came behind like a shepherdess herding her flock, fussing around until Thomas was served and then sending the servants away again.

Thomas speared a fresh piece of heron, spiced with cinnamon and vinegar. "I'm glad you persuaded me to stay, Margaret. It will be some time before I eat a meal as tasty as this one." He held out his cup for more wine, his eyes sparkling appreciatively. "If only I dared to take an open stand against Richard. How much easier I would feel." He shook his head. "He has me trapped and hobbled, holding my son as he does."

"Be careful, Thomas, I would never forgive myself if anything happened to Lord Strange, because of me."

"I intend to be careful, Margaret. But then am I not always careful?" He smiled ruefully. "The trouble is that Richard knows my nature too well. I must pray that he will stay his hand." He shrugged his broad shoulders. "I don't even know what side I will take myself."

Margaret looked directly at him. "So you say, my lord, but I believe different. Would you sit here with me if you intended to fight for Richard?"

"I'll leave the answer for you to judge." He stood up, his eyes twinkling. "I'd better have some sleep before I ride out again. Do not let me lie too long in my bed, I might just miss the battle altogether!"

She helped him off with his boots and tucked the covers around him as if he were a child; he was a rock of a man, wise and cunning, but his strength was undeniable.

"But don't you see, Thomas, I must be there!" Margaret pulled the plain cloak more firmly around her slender shoulders.

"It is unheard of!" Thomas was almost spluttering in his anger. "A woman at the battlefield? Ridiculous!"

"It is not all that ridiculous, Thomas," Margaret said mildly. "After all, Queen Margaret of Anjou went into battle like a man."

"That is a different matter," Thomas said sharply. "For one thing the Queen wasn't my wife. And so I had no control over her actions."

"Please, Thomas, I will stay far enough away to keep out of danger. And Elizabeth will come with me. I'll be quite safe."

He took her hands. "Margaret, I will not be able to stay near you. We do not know even where the battle will take place, if it ever does!"

"There will certainly be a battle, Thomas, you know it as well as I do. The King is not going to allow my son to ride unchallenged on to English soil."

He sighed in exasperation. "What if the battle should go to Richard? You will have no chance of hiding away. You will be taken immediately."

Margaret regarded him steadily. "If the battle should be lost, I will not care what becomes of me."

"But I will care." He slapped his hands to his sides. "How can I concentrate on strategy if I am worried over you? Please, Margaret, say you will stay quietly at home."

Elizabeth snorted inelegantly. "It's no good, my lord. If Margaret has made up her mind to ride with you, she will do so!"

"All right!" Thomas waved his hands in resignation. "Come, if you must." He shook his head. "But on one condition. You must ride behind my men, at a good distance; and flee if there is any danger."

"I agree to your terms, Thomas," Margaret

said, smiling, and stood on tiptoe to kiss his cheek.

"It will not be as easy as you imagine," Thomas warned. "We will be riding through the night. Your horse could stumble and throw you."

"And pigs could fly to the moon," Margaret said, her spirits high now that she had won her own way.

"Come, then, we will start out before the sun sinks too low in the sky. Otherwise, my dear Margaret, it will all be over without us even having a scent of the action."

The evening air was cool, with the heavy scents of summer drifting across the fields. Margaret, with Elizabeth at her side, stayed as Thomas had commanded, well away from the large company of soldiers.

"Soon all that I have hoped for will be accomplished." Margaret looked up at the reddening sky. "And it looks as if even the sun will be on our side."

Elizabeth shifted uncomfortably in the saddle. "I am feeling as fat and heavy as an overfed boar, Margaret," she said plaintively.

"Is that all you have to say on the evening of my triumph?"

Margaret hid a smile. Elizabeth had grown plump, there was no denying of it. She certainly was not the thin lithe girl who had once been able to climb down from a high window and flee from the rebels who were marching on London.

That was all such a long time ago.

"Why so silent?" Elizabeth looked at her hard, her forehead wrinkled crossly. "You are laughing at my discomfort, you heartless woman!"

"No, indeed," Margaret spoke with difficulty. "I am not laughing; I was remembering the time when you and I climbed out of a high window. What courage we had then."

"Foolhardiness!" Elizabeth said firmly. "And this is just as silly and dangerous. Following an army into battle, indeed! Who has ever heard of such a thing!"

"Come now," Margaret stifled her mirth. "I can see that really and truly you are enjoying every moment of it. It is a long time since we have had such an adventure."

"If you ask me, I must need my head examined to be here at all. At my age I should be tucked up in a warm comfortable bed, not riding around the countryside like this."

"But just think what a tale you will have to tell when it is all over. You will be the most sought after lady in England."

"That is if I am alive to tell any sort of tale at all," Elizabeth said drily.

"You are determined to grouse, I can see." Margaret spurred her horse forward. "So I will give you some solitude, if that is what will appease you."

"No!" Elizabeth said quickly. "I don't want to be left alone. Who knows what sort of creature might be lurking in the trees waiting to pounce on me."

Margaret laughed out loud. "All right, I will stay near you. We will probably stop for a rest soon, anyway."

"I certainly hope so." Elizabeth shifted her position yet again. "I will no doubt fall from this creature. I will not be able to stand, that is certain." She looked at Margaret, her face suddenly grown serious. "All my grousings are just so much mist in the sun," she said. "Really my heart beats fast and my head grows dizzy when I think of how much this means to you."

Margaret leaned over and touched her shoulder. "Do you think I do not know that? I have known you too long and too well to think otherwise."

They rode in silence for a moment with the clip-crop of the horses' hooves on the hard road for company. The sun had disappeared completely, and the sky had turned to silver.

"My son," Margaret said softly. "I will see my son again when the sun rises in the sky. God and all the saints will protect him. What will happen was meant to be from the very beginning. From the moment he was born. Henry Tudor will rule wisely. He will make England prosperous, and he will bring peace to all men."

Her words fell into the stillness of the night, echoing along the valleys and rising to the hilltops like the words of a prayer.

The hillside was still and silent in the night air

and deep purple shadows lay like pools flung down from the skies. Margaret reined her horse and slipped from the saddle, ignoring the stiffness of her legs and the ache in her back.

Elizabeth was not so quiet in her movements. She grunted heavily, almost falling to her knees as her feet touched the earth.

"I wasn't built for this sort of adventure," she said breathlessly.

Margaret felt her whole body grow taut with tension. She tried to pierce the gloom with her eyes, but beyond the hillside nothing moved.

"I am so frightened!" Margaret was hardly aware that she had uttered the words out loud until Elizabeth touched her arm.

"I think it would be better if we were to hide the horses and go forward on foot," she whispered.

Margaret nodded. "Perhaps you are right. It would be unwise to declare our presence." She looked up at the sky. "I hardly think the battle will begin during the hours of darkness, but one cannot be sure of that."

"Look there, Margaret!" Elizabeth was suddenly excited. "I can see the torches from the camp. My Lord Stanley must have decided to rest for a time."

"In that case we shall make our way to him, and wait for morning in his company. A far better prospect than walking alone in the darkness."

Carefully, they led their horses towards the flickering lights.

"They are further ahead of us than I thought." Margaret suddenly felt an overwhelming weariness. It was an effort to place one foot in front of the other.

Elizabeth sensed her feelings and caught her arm.

"Do not falter now. Your moment of glory is almost here."

Margaret stopped walking and covered her face with her hands. "I feel cold with fear. What if I see my son die as Margaret of Anjou watched the execution of her only child? I feel I cannot bear to go on."

"Have courage, Margaret. You have waited so long for this day."

Margaret swayed for a moment and held on to the bridle in an effort to steady herself. "What if my faith was misplaced, and I've been wrong all these years? I may have led my son into his own death trap."

"That is silly talk," Elizabeth said briskly. "I would not have come with you if I'd thought you were going to give way to the vapours."

Margaret took a deep breath, making a visible effort to control her emotions.

"You know the cause is a just one," Elizabeth continued. "King Henry the Sixth himself foretold of your son's rise to the throne of England."

The sound of hooves approaching silenced both of them. They stood mute and afraid until they recognised the rider as Thomas Stanley.

"Come with me," he said briskly. "We can do

nothing until the light of day spreads over the land." He lifted Margaret's face to his. "Not regretting the journey, are you? If so, I can give you a guard of soldiers to take you to the nearest village. Market Bosworth is just a few miles away."

"No!" Margaret's denial was sharp. "I do not regret following you. I must stay. Whatever happens, I will be here near at hand."

"A few hours sleep will refresh us all." Thomas took the reins of her mount and led him carefully over the stony ground.

But Margaret could not sleep. She passed the hours of night on her knees, disregarding the stiffness of her limbs from the long hours riding.

At last, the cold fingers of dawn stretched across the sky, bringing life to the trees and turning the grass from silver to a lush green.

Thomas had been awake before her and she saw him arrayed in his armour like some unfamiliar giant.

"It looks as if we chose our spot with wisdom, Margaret," he said with forced heartiness. "My outriders have seen both armies approaching Redmore plain, just over the meadow, there."

Margaret shivered a little in spite of the warmth of the rising sun.

"You would be better over there to the left, Margaret, near that clump of trees," he smiled at her. "Have faith in me, my dear. I will make my move when the time is right."

He left her then, and with a sinking heart she

watched his army move away across the country-side.

Elizabeth was scarcely awake. "What is happening, Margaret? Has the fighting begun?"

Margaret shook her head. "We must withdraw and take up a stand over there, on that small rise. We can hide the horses further back among the woods."

Her hands shook, but Margaret appeared calm as in silence she led the way across the woodland.

"Look, Margaret!" Elizabeth shouted and Margaret spun round, her heart in her throat.

"Richard's standard." Elizabeth pointed excitedly. "Over there, Margaret. See how it flutters in the breeze."

They hurried to the small hillock and Margaret was almost afraid to look back over the plain. She wished in that instant that she could stop the armies approaching each other, but it was too late to think like that now.

Elizabeth climbed with difficulty into the saddle in order to see more clearly, and Margaret closed her eyes, sending a silent prayer to the saints for the protection of her son.

The hot August sun beat down on her upturned face and the still air was suddenly rent with the cries of hundreds of voices.

Reluctantly Margaret turned towards the plain which had suddenly become black with soldiers. She shuddered, hearing the ring of steel and the agonised cry of the wounded as they fell beneath the flying hooves of the horses.

"Look!" Elizabeth said loudly. "I can see my Lord Stanley's army. They are holding aloof beyond the plain. Why doesn't he do something?"

Margaret pulled herself up into the saddle and looked to where Elizabeth was pointing.

"He is afraid," she said softly, "for his son's life. And who am I to condemn him when I share his anguish?"

The noise grew louder and Elizabeth cried in fear as it seemed for a moment that some of the horsemen were making towards them. They turned and raced back into the mass of men and horses, and Elizabeth sighed in relief.

"Do you think we had better withdraw, Margaret?" she said hesitantly. "I never expected it to be anything as horrible as this."

Margaret shook her head. "You go if you wish. I could no more leave this spot as take up arms myself." She gave Elizabeth a quick glance. "I have no right to expect you to endure this with me."

"If you stay, then so shall I," said Elizabeth stoutly, though her face had turned ashen, and her hands shook as they clutched at the reins of the frightened horse.

Margaret lost all idea of time. She sat watching the scene before her, almost in a dream. There was no way of telling which side was gaining the ascendancy. Indeed, it seemed to Margaret that no one could escape from that terrible battle alive. She saw a fresh rush of men join the fighting and realised with a shock of fear that Thomas had at last decided which side he was on. She hoped and prayed that she was right in believing he was for her son.

She seemed to sink into a daze. The sun beat down fiercely and the noise had gone on for ever. She wondered if there would ever be peace in the land again. She thought of Edmund, her first and only true love, and of the kindly Stafford. He had cared for her well. She saw young Charles Somerset and knew that if Henry Tudor came out of this battle victorious, Charles would never want for anything again.

She forced herself to open her eyes, becoming slowly aware that the terrible noise was dying away. Was it possible that the battle was at last over?

She urged her mount forward nearer to the plain, disregarding Elizabeth's frantic exhortations for her to come back out of harm's way.

Something glinted in the sun. It was the crown of England held aloft! Her breath caught in her throat as she watched it being placed on hair that was like a flame under the richness of the crown. Her son, this tall young man, was now the King of England.

Someone waved to her as she slipped from her horse and stood transfixed with joy on the edge of the field. And then there were horsemen riding towards her.

She had eyes only for the straight, upright

young man who was jumping from his horse and taking her in his arms.

"Mother, this is the proudest moment of my life," he said. "I am overjoyed that you are here to share it with me."

She clung to him, blinded with tears, and Thomas smiled at her over Henry Tudor's broad shoulder.

"I chose my time wisely, Margaret. Lord Strange is alive and well."

She had never experienced such happiness. It shimmered through her like hot gold running in her veins.

"My son, the King of England!" She dropped a curtsey, and smiling, he drew her to her feet.

For a moment it was as if Edmund stood before her, young and strong as when they'd first met. Then her vision cleared and she saw that it was her son clasping her hands.

Her tears fell on to their twined fingers, and lay shimmering like jewels, more precious than any to be found on earth.

We hope you have enjoyed this Large Print book. Other G.K. Hall & Co. or Chivers Press Large Print books are available at your library or directly from the publishers.

For more information about current and up-coming titles, please call or write, without obligation, to:

G.K. Hall & Co.
P.O. Box 159
Thorndike, Maine 04986 USA
Tel. (800) 257-5157

OR

Chivers Press Limited
Windsor Bridge Road
Bath BA2 3AX
England
Tel. (0225) 335336

All our Large Print titles are designed for easy reading, and all our books are made to last.